---- ★ ----

ABOVE SUSPICION?

With a faint feeling that made the hair on his head prickle, Coffin got the first intimation that even if it was not his case, he himself was in it.

Right in it.

He was seeing it all so differently; he was seeing it from the other side of the mirror.

And he was looking at his own face.

Of course Jordan was taking time off to talk to him, and of course he was observed, probably on all sides.

It was his house.

That investigating team he'd talked about, they were probably passionately interested in him.

In the nicest possible way, of course. Young Coffin? Decent chap, this business can't be anything to do with him. Still, we'd better look.

You bet.

He wiped his forehead.

Hot. Was it getting hotter?

---- ★ ----

COFFIN IN FASHION

Gwendoline Butler

WORLDWIDE.

TORONTO • NEW YORK • LONDON
AMSTERDAM • PARIS • SYDNEY • HAMBURG
STOCKHOLM • ATHENS • TOKYO • MILAN
MADRID • WARSAW • BUDAPEST • AUCKLAND

COFFIN IN FASHION

A Worldwide Mystery/July 1992

First published by St. Martin's Press Incorporated.

ISBN 0-373-26100-4

Printed in U.S.A.

COFFIN IN FASHION

ONE

ONE DAY in the middle of the 1960s, John Coffin, then a detective-sergeant but hopeful of promotion, made what his solicitor assured him was the best investment of his life: he bought a house. He was proud of himself as he signed the cheque, which represented a lot of borrowed money.

'The best thing you've ever done,' said the young solicitor, just married and a new householder himself. 'A good investment. Property there will go up and up.'

'Think so? All I could afford.' Not even that, really.

'Mouncy Street might be a bit run down now, took a pasting during the war, but it will go up and up. I've bought round there myself, as a matter of fact. Rowley Road. Worth every penny you've paid.'

He'd have to believe that, thought Coffin cynically, if he's in Rowley Road. If anything, Rowley Road was a bit seedier than dear old Mouncy Street. 'A lot to do to the place.' He would do most of it himself, though, and only get help with what he couldn't manage. He could wield a paintbrush but he was no carpenter.

'A sound investment,' said young Mr Davenport.

Later, Coffin felt like telling the lawyer what he had actually got for his money.

Death. Murder. A love-affair. A family inheritance. How did that rate in the profit and loss account?

The district of Mouncy Street and Decimus Street, together with Paradise Street and Rowley Road, was known to Coffin of old. He had gone to Hook Road Senior Boys' School, which wasn't so far away, and had chalked slogans on the wall of the factory which was now Belmodes and made clothes, and had bought ice-cream in the little café now called The Coffee Shop and under the new management of an ambiguous character called Cat.

He slipped the house keys in his pocket and went to have a look at his new home.

He stood in the hall and looked around. From the front door you could see through the living-room to the kitchen and then up the stairs to the lavatory.

It smelt damp. Well, it smelt. A lot of living had been done in this house, and it showed.

There was a shabby raincoat and a cap hanging on a peg on the scullery door, left behind by the last occupant. A breeze through a broken windowpane lifted the sleeve so that an arm seemed to wave at him.

Suddenly he felt so depressed that he had to go round to the Red Anchor and have a drink. There he found his patron and mentor, Commander Dander, CID, drinking a double whisky.

'I've had a psychic experience,' Coffin said. 'That bloody house is haunted.'

'Who by?'

'By an old man with a hat on.'

'You need a whisky,' said Dander, who always took this cure himself. 'Or a woman.' That was his other remedy.

GABRIEL GLASS knew John Coffin by sight because every morning for the last few weeks they had met at the same bus stop. Gabriel had been so christened by her mother, who said that was the name she desired for her daughter and that Archangels were sexless anyway. Her mother had invented Unisex long before anyone else. So all her life Gabriel had been in contest with her name. She was definitely a girl herself. But looking back, she wondered if her name had not contributed its own small share to the murders in Mouncy Street. Another sexual ambiguity, anyway, to add to that already murky soup. Gabriel got off the No. 36 bus while Coffin got on, and she noticed him because she always noticed attractive men. But she thought he looked worried.

He was worried.

Today workmen were coming to replace the rafters in the attic and replace rotten floorboards in the kitchen. He hoped they would get on with the work fast without too many tea-breaks, and then go. He had owned his house for nearly two months now and he was still camping out in it. Progress must be made soon. It was tiring and the police work he was engaged on, undercover and complex, needed all the energy he could give it.

Gabriel pondered what job he did; he looked efficient but anxious. She concluded his work was important to him and exacting, something very nearly, but not quite, beyond his powers. Since this was her own state exactly, she knew how he felt. Sometimes she felt as stretched as an elastic band.

Now he went one way and she went another. Wherever he was going (and one day she'd find out), she was going to Belmodes Factory where she worked. Later she would take a taxi to Beauchamp Place. The day would come when she would go in a Rolls. Her own.

Her mind reverted to her own troubles, most of which centred around Rose Hilaire, owner of Belmodes and of the shop in Beauchamp Place. Also of other desirable properties like a Porsche car (not what Gabriel would have gone for), and some good jewellery. She had a shop in Knightsbridge, another in Bond Street, a fourth in Sloane Street and yet another in Baker Street. This small chain of exclusive shops was all fed from Belmodes in Greenwich.

At the moment she was tired. For the last few months she had been working hard for her boss, and even harder at a project of her own. She had this little private scheme going with her good friend Charley Moon, the young photographer, whose South London studio was in an old stable belonging to Belmodes.

She turned into Mouncy Street. It was a quiet, working class street of houses, some in a better state of repair than others. It was the sort of street that seemed respectable by day, but which you didn't fancy too much at night.

Behind Hook Road School, in an area bounded by the main road and Mouncy Street to the west, was a club for dancing and drinking called Tiger's. There had never been a tiger present, but in the 1930s a travelling circus had rested in the park for a week. Tiger's was partly owned by a man called Joe Landau, who had also put money into Belmodes, which Rose was sweating to pay off. His partner was a local business-man who kept a shop, liked to live a quiet life and not worry his mother who was an invalid.

A lot of troublesome people poured out of Tiger's after dark, as Gabriel knew. She had been there with Charley and summed up the customers as ready for anything. 'Living on the edge, that lot.'

Perhaps she was imaginative, but some weeks, af-ter one of her long sessions with Charley, she'd treated herself to a taxi home (not a frequent indulgence in her hard-working life); she had looked out of her window and seen a woman walking down the gutters.

Walking. Stopping. Then walking again. Finally the woman had sat on a wall outside a house.

With a shock she had recognized her employer, Rose Hilaire. She could hardly believe her eyes. What was Rose up to? Was she drunk or ill?

Gabriel had leaned forward to ask the taxi-driver what he made of it, but he said he'd seen nothing and no one. She was pretty sure he had, which made it seem worse.

Next day Rose had seemed normal, although pale, but she had said nothing, and Gabriel had certainly not mentioned it.

After all, she had her own secret to keep. Moreover, she was resentful of Rose Hilaire.

'I could kill that woman. Easily. Be a pleasure.'

Charley Moon disliked this. 'Don't talk so much about death and killing,' he had said. 'I don't like to hear it. Worries me.' At this time in their relationship they often quarrelled. Partly because they had known each other for a long time and could afford to be cross with each other, and partly because they were both restless and unhappy.

'She's holding me back.'

'She's run that shop of hers and this factory for years. She must know what she's about.'

'I'm in a straitjacket . . . I design the clothes. She takes all the credit, and she pays me peanuts.'

'She knows the market. Her market.'

A market of comfortably off ladies who could afford to pay high prices but did not move in circles which demanded couture clothes. 'Pretend' couture, echoes of Paris and Milan, were more their line. These Rose Hilaire provided.

But the market was changing. Fashion was becoming bright, crisp and street-orientated. For the moment high fashion was casual-chic and even Rose Hilaire's ladies were noticing.

Gabriel got off the bus at the corner of Mouncy Street, looked hungrily at the ham rolls in the delicatessen, remembered her diet and swung off towards the factory. Her skirt was mid-thigh and met her boots on the way up. Both skirt and boots were soft white leather, cuffed with suede. She passed the chemist's shop and then turned back to buy some aspirin. It looked as though it was going to be that sort of day. Harry Lindsay handed her what she wanted across the counter without a word. One of his silent days. He was into silence. [He'd been blown up during the war as a small boy, and people said it made him sad. But Gabriel attributed it to the perpetual presence of his invalid mother.] He was also into late-nineteenth-century interiors of genuine old-fashioned chemists' shops, and high stiff collars on his shirt to go with it.

The sunlight filtered through the great red, green and yellow jars standing in his window, not many of them about now, and coloured his face and cheeks with bands of colour.

By the end of the day she had been grateful for the aspirin but her head still banged. She popped another aspirin in her mouth and followed it with coffee. Was the man at the bus stop ending the day with a headache? He looked as though he knew what pain was. But pain came in different parcels for everyone.

'If I tried to kill old Rose, that cow, what method would you suggest, Charley?'

'Shift your head.' Charley did not want to pursue the theme. 'To the left.' He was setting up the lights above her head, checking what he saw in the lens, getting ready to photograph her.

Occasionally she acted as a model for Charley if he was hard up, but this time it was for her.

This was her very own collection of clothes, a deep secret from Rose Hilaire who owned Gabriel body and soul, or thought she did, and which Gaby meant to use as a launching-pad for herself. Strictly under the rose, of course, since according to her contract all work done by Gabriel belonged to Rose.

Charley was photographing the clothes for a portfolio she was going to send out, and in the interests of economy she was modelling them herself.

'Don't talk for a moment, and don't even breathe.'
Charley adjusted a screen behind her. 'I don't know
why you bother with all this. You're a beautiful girl.
Why not settle for a rich husband?'

Gabriel ignored this sally, she and Charley had
known each other since art school and his remarks
could be passed over. Or bitterly contested, according
to how she felt. He did the same in return. 'Do you
know what she said to me today?' It had been the fi-
nal insult. 'She said: "My customers aren't dolly birds
but ladies so please remember that, even if you can't
be one yourself." That was because she heard Dolly
ask me if I was on the Pill. And *then* I heard her on the
phone telling Lady Olney that the new blue tunic dress
would take ten years off her.'

Charley squinted through his lens. 'All right, so she
exploits you. For my money you fight on equal
weights. Look at what you're doing now.'

'Blur my face out, won't you, so she won't know it's
me if she sees the album,' said Gabriel apprehen-
sively.

'She'll find out in the end.'

'But it'll slow her down. All I need is time.' These
designs were as good as she thought they were. She
crossed her fingers for luck.

'She'll kill you.'

'No. Just snitch the designs. Let her try.'

'I bet she could sue you.'

'And I bet she won't. She'd have to admit in open court that the designs for the last two years were mine and nothing but mine.'

For a while they worked, Gabriel rapidly changing clothes; she had made every dress with her own hands, cutting and stitching, and she knew exactly how to wear them.

The photograph session was taking place in Charley's South London studio which was in the loft of an old stable attached to Belmodes. Rose Hilaire was, in fact, his landlady. She also owned, although he did not know it, the terrace house in Mouncy Street which he was considering renting, and another she had already sold. Meanwhile, Charley was camping out in his studio which he was renovating himself. At present he was working on the splendid oak floors, sanding and polishing them. When life got too uncomfortable he stayed with a friend he had living in the district. Or, at odd times, he slept in the van he kept in the access road between Mouncy Street and Decimus Street.

Finally Charley said: 'That's it. Let's dismantle the show.' He started to take down his lights. 'I think she'll beat you: she's got armour plate all round her.'

Slowly Gabriel said: 'She's got one big hole in that armour.'

They looked at each other.

'You mean the boy?' said Charley in a low voice.

Gabriel nodded. 'That *sad* boy.'

Sadness might be infectious, perhaps it had spread from Rose Hilaire to her son, emptying his eyes and his mind, a kind of family infection that might spread outwards to Gabriel herself.

Another reason for getting away. Bad luck did brush off so, everyone knew that.

'Do you think he might kill her?' He's only a kid, Gabriel thought, for heaven's sake what are you saying? But she had said it. And not such a kid. Fourteen, wasn't he?

'Oh no. It wouldn't be like that.' Charley sounded as if he knew.

'Do you think *she* might kill him?'

Charley shook his head. 'Oh no. Not because I think neither are capable of it. Anyone could be—but because there has to be love to kill.'

'SHE'S UP TO something.' The speaker was a tall sturdy woman with a crest of bright golden hair just turning grey. She was wearing her coat ready to go home. 'Rose, I'm telling you. Am I your friend or am I not?' A waft of garlic sped across her employer's desk.

Rose Hilaire, born Rose Lee, once married, and mother of Steve, whose whole life was hidden, unspoken and out of sight, an underground boy. She firmly believed that he was in no way different, that tucked inside him was a mental giant, but he just WOULD NOT SPEAK. Not to her. Sometimes he wouldn't even look, only turned his head away to stare at the wall. She knew he understood, though; she could see. Oddly enough he performed well at school even though in an average kind of way. Whatever Steve was he was not average, she told his teacher so. And of course she never mentioned that he would not talk to her.

Sometimes, at bad moments, she thought he liked her new motorcar, the Porsche, more than her, and that if anything happened to her, he would find it a good mother substitute. She had caught him sitting at the wheel, playing with the gears. He'd even tried to drive it away.

In anger, she'd hit him, and then was ashamed because you never hit your child. So she'd promised to give him driving lessons, on the quiet, when no one could see. But the anger was still there between them, this time it had transferred itself to him. It came out in the way he held the wheel, as if the car was his anger and his weapon. This frightened her. So she'd dropped the driving instruction. It was illegal, anyway.

At that moment, the end of her working day, the day after Gabriel's photo session, her mind was about equally divided between Gabriel, whom she knew to be a problem but did not yet know how big a one, and Steve. Here again, was he a real problem or just a tiny little one that she had let get out of hand?

One day, she thought, he will walk out of this house and I will never see him again. Fourteen years old and already she felt she was writing his obituary. Only underground boys like Steve did not have obituaries, they just wandered off and one day there was a tiny paragraph in the daily paper about a boy being found. Or perhaps not even that. Just silence for evermore. But silence was what she had now.

One day she might find out why he hated her, if that was what it was, and not some family sickness to which she might one day succumb herself. But no, the bad blood was on his father's side of the family.

At this moment she had a letter in her desk from Steve's teacher praising his dramatic ability and suggesting he ought to go to theatre school. Rose thought she knew all about his dramatic powers, having been only too often a reluctant witness.

Although he would not talk to her, Steve had no intention of going short of his needs and he could mime. He could get across what he wanted all right and Rose never had any difficulty in being convinced he meant it. She wondered if he really wanted to go to drama school? So far he had made no such signal to her, which probably indicated he had no such intention. On the other hand, sometimes he liked to keep her in the dark until the last possible moment.

Small wonder that with such a training in body language she had no difficulty in reading Gabriel's mind:

she knew that Gabriel was keeping something from her, could make a pretty good guess what it was and did not, in spite of what Gabriel might think, even mind very much. She had a simple philosophy of all being fair... and the rag trade was a kind of war. She even liked Gabriel, but that didn't mean she would let her get away with anything. Far, far from it.

'I'll kill that girl if she really screws me up.'

She was older than Gabriel, but not as much older as Gabriel thought. Nevertheless, in her career she had seen a good many Gabriels come and go. Some had more talent than others and stayed the course better. Character came into it too, you needed toughness in this trade. Gabriel was one of the smartest and the most talented. Perhaps the most talented. Rose respected that talent even while she knew very well that Gabriel would not stay with her for ever, or even for much longer. But while she was under contract, Rose meant her to abide by it.

Unluckily, she herself had no creative talent worth of talking of. She had a good head for business combined with an intuitive grasp of what the market wanted. In other words, she understood fashion as interpreter. She needed someone like Gabriel and meant to hang to her if she could. Usually she was content to let her young designers drift away; few of them were heard of again. Perhaps contact with Rose Hilaire had sucked them dry. But in the case of Gabriel she could foresee a long and profitable relationship, if not a particularly happy one. If Gabriel examined the small print of her contract she could see that Rose had allowed herself a ten-year option on her services.

Now she said: 'I don't trust her, Dagmar, but thanks all the same.'

Dagmar Blond buttoned her coat. 'How long have we known each other?'

Rose did not answer because she knew from experience that Dagmar was about to tell her.

'I worked for your aunt when she was running the business, and I was with your grandfather before that, God rest his soul.'

Grandfather Hilaire's soul received frequent benedictions from Dagmar Blond who found him a useful seal of approval, although in life she had been no more than an errand girl in his workshop whose face he barely knew. Still, it proved she went a long way back with Rose.

'So we inherited each other.' Rose remained good-humoured. 'And if I remember right, Gabriel came with an introduction from you.'

'All right, all right. She came from Paradise Street. That ought to have told you something.'

Paradise Street was a short, crowded street running between Mouncy Street and Rowley Road, near the railway station and hard by the factory. It was famous for the close-knit family groups which lived there. Famous also for living by their own rules, and being well known to the police.

'So did we once,' said Rose Hilaire, 'and we've moved away. That girl will be going a long way from Paradise Street.'

But they both knew you never got Paradise Street out of your system; it was there for always, something you were born to, like a crown or an inherited disease.

It said something about you when you said you came from Paradise Street. It had a past and a history, had Paradise Street, and they both projected themselves into the future. Strange violent things had happened there and were suppressed by the inhabitants: it was their business, other people could only guess.

'I can manage her,' Rose repeated.

'And what about Joe?'

'Joe?'

'Yes. Joseph Benedict Landau,' said Dagmar. 'Can you manage him?'

'Leave Joe out of it.' Rose did not like to hear Dagmar talk about Joe; he was private.

She and Gabriel represented opposing poles in fashion but Rose was old enough to know that in the end they might complement each other. Even in looks they were different: Gabriel, besides being still very young, was slight, small-boned like a bird, and with dark eyes and flow of dark hair, which, at the moment, she ironed straight every morning. To those who said she might be bald at forty as a consequence she said she did not expect to live that long or else that she would buy a wig. Already she owned two falls of hair which she wore on an Alice band. Rose was tall, full of bust and narrow of waist, with a round face and strong curly blonde hair. Like Gabriel, she had a wardrobe of wigs. On her they never looked quite natural.

She looked at the clock on her desk, a round black face set in a crystal block, one of her first presents to herself when she began to make money. The factory was closing down, emptying for the night, but she often worked late, telephoning round her branches or to various contacts in the fashion trade. It was her time for keeping in touch with movements in her world.

But she also liked to be home to greet Steve when he came in from school. He came as near as he ever did to talking to her then. Anyway, it was the time that messages passed back and forth between them.

Because she wanted to stay in the neighbourhood from which she sprang, a desire reinforced by her wish to give a strong background to Steve, she had moved to a flat in a new block overlooking the river not far from Mouncy Street. She could walk there in ten minutes, but she drove in her Porsche. She was a slow and cautious driver, causing both alarm and irritation to other drivers by her handling of her fast car.

She wanted to get home but she also had several business matters she needed to check up on, not least of which was the possible destination of the portfolio of designs she imagined that Gabriel was creating. You couldn't keep that sort of thing a secret in the relatively tight world they lived in. Only as youthful an operator as Gabriel could have expected to.

On looking the field over, it seemed to Rose that there were two candidates: on the one hand there was the old-established firm of Senlis Styles which was seeking (and rightly so in Rose's opinion) to change its image. On the other hand there was the small and thrusting new firm of Lizzie Dreamer whose super-active boss, a stout young man called Touch, was busy scooping up all the new talent available.

Rose herself had had a brush or two with Teddy Touch and almost wished Gabriel joy of him, but this was a weakness she could not allow herself. You hang on to what you had and you never let go, that was her style.

Then the telephone rang on her desk, not the red one that was entirely office and work, but the blue one which was her private number. Only family and friends used it.

'Hello. Is that you?'

A young, gruff voice, she knew it at once, even though it was so rarely used for her.

'Steve, what is it? Why are you calling?'

'Well . . .' A hesitation, a fumbling for words. Was it that he could not speak, or would not? 'Just to say— that something bad has happened.'

'Steve . . . Please . . . What is it?' She was almost shouting.

The telephone was removed from his hand, and another voice spoke. A woman's voice, educated, gentle but with a hint of command and slight Scottish accent. 'Miss Fraser speaking . . .' Steve's headmistress at Hook Road School.

'Yes, I know.'

'Can you come round, Mrs Hilaire? At once? I think it would be best. There is something you have to be told.'

It seemed to Rose Hilaire that she could hear other voices in the background. Another woman and perhaps a man.

Yes, certainly a man, and why not, in a school? But all the same she didn't like the sound of it at all.

Before she left she picked up her blue phone. 'Joe? I'm sorry, darling. Tonight's not on. Trouble here.'

HOOK ROAD SCHOOL had lately undergone a face-lift. As cosmetic surgery, it was minor and superficial, designed as is usually the case with such surgery to raise the spirits rather than change the character. Old woodwork had been replaced with newer structures, strip lighting had taken the place of glass globes hanging from the ceiling. Pale turquoise paint had replaced the steady old green paint of the old days. A new heating system boosted the temperature so that some rooms were uncomfortably warm, though the lavatories and washrooms for both staff and children were as chilly and damp as ever. Within the next decade the buildings were due to be demolished to give place to a glittering new palace of stone and glass. The staff had seen pictures of it and were profoundly uneasy.

But for the moment Hook Road School was much as it had been when the Victorian School Board of Governors devised its architecture and meant it to last. As indeed it had done, through two world wars, Zeppelin raids and the Blitz. The ghosts of the old pupils (who still seemed to hang about in the smells and noises) would have felt quite at home.

There was a piano being played somewhere in the building; there had always been a piano being played.

Miss Fraser shut the door against the noise. She was young for a headmistress, and as tough as her job demanded, which was tough enough. She gave the impression of having an active and vital life outside school. Otherwise she was fond of children and good-humoured. But today she looked tense and preoccupied, as if underneath she was frightened.

In the room with her was a bearded man, sitting down, a uniformed policewoman, standing up, and Steve Hilaire who was half sitting, half crouched on a hard chair, beside him his sports bag.

'Come in, Mrs Hilaire.' Miss Fraser took her hand away from the door, and momentarily leaned against it as if she could do with its support. 'Let me get you a chair. Steve, get one for your mother.'

Silently Steve got off his chair for his mother to sit down. Their eyes met and passed each other without comment. Rose's gaze slid on and settled on the policewoman.

'What's this? Why is she here?' Rose, when frightened, was always aggressive.

The policewoman looked at Miss Fraser, who gave a slight nod. They settled it between them that Miss Fraser would do the talking. At first.

Rose's eyes flicked nervously to Steve. 'What's it about, then? Why am I here? What's it to do with Steve?'

She couldn't stop her eyes going back to that bag of his.

'This afternoon,' began Lovella Fraser, 'the school had its uniform inspection, there's always one once a term. Just a check-up to see that everyone has the right shoes, and blazer and so. Sports equipment, that sort of thing. Every child lays out his stuff, and we do it form by form.' She nodded towards the bearded man. 'Mr Gordon is Steve's form-master.'

'So what's the mystery?' Rose was getting her nerve back. 'Steve—you haven't taken anything that doesn't belong to you?' At times of pressure the old Paradise Street slipped out; petty theft had been an occupation there, and accusations of it a commonplace of life.

'No, we don't think he's taken anything.'

'Come on, then. Why am I here?'

Miss Fraser cleared her throat, she was still to do the talking. 'I don't know if you have heard about Ephraim Humphreys?'

Rose stared at her, she appeared to be searching her memory. 'I don't know.' She frowned, temporarily off balance. 'Ephraim Humphreys . . . ? He's a boy, a little boy?'

The policewoman made an involuntary move. Young, yes, still a boy, aged twelve. But not so little. Tall for his age. Above average. Steve was tall also, although his choirboy-like, innocent face sometimes made you forget this.

'I don't read the papers much,' Rose stumbled on.

Miss Fraser accepted the tacit admission that Rose knew more than she seemed capable of getting out. 'Yes. It has been in the newspapers.'

'He's gone away?' Her gaze fell upon Steve's sports bag, her Christmas present to him and now on the headmistress's desk. Open.

The woman detective thought: Gone away was one way of putting it. Two weeks ago a twelve-year-old boy called Ephraim Humphreys, a pupil at Hook Road School, left his family home after a sparse breakfast in good time to do his paper round and then get to school... The woman detective shifted her stance from one foot to another.

'No one knows if he ever got here, his papers were delivered but no one noticed if he arrived at school or not.'

'I'm remembering,' said Rose. It had all happened at a time when she was busier than usual getting together the winter collection of clothes. They made four collections a year, as did most wholesalers (and in spite of her chain of shops, that was how she regarded herself; she wasn't a couture house, that was sure). The winter collection, the third for which Gabriel had been responsible, had been a difficult one. Skirts were going up, getting shorter and shorter, but there were hints that daytime overcoats might suddenly lengthen, sweeping the ground. At least one Paris house had shown some such, and one New York. In New York they had, as they say, bombed. But who could say what London would do? London took its own line, it was on its own. Rose had wanted to stay with a safe, half-way line and Gabriel had said that was disaster, you had to be brave and plunge. Literally, let the hemline of heavyweight winter coats drop, go right down to the ground. Team them with short, short skirts and wet-look shiny boots, and you would have a total look. Gabriel loved to talk about total looks. It had been their first big quarrel. Gabriel had won.

Into their quarrel the story about the local boy who had gone missing had hardly penetrated, but she found now she could dig out more details than she would have guessed. It was all there, a story waiting to tell itself to her.

The boy had gone out from his home in Decimus Street after eating a bowl of ready-cook porridge and drinking a cup of tea. He had been wearing his usual school clothes, but on his feet his favourite but eccentric red boots. These had been a present from his grandmother in America. He loved them and always wore them when he could. They had a soft canvas top and leather bindings, a kind of house slipper really, and not for outdoors. He would have to change them when he got to school because they were not allowed with the school uniform.

He had not been missed until the late afternoon when his mother came in from work; she thought he might be playing with friends and waited. When her husband arrived they both took alarm. They tried asking friends and neighbours but no one had seen

Ephraim. The husband (who was not the boy's father) went round the streets looking for the boy, the wife stayed home, waiting in case her son came back. Next day they discovered he had never been at school. But by that time the police already knew and were on the job.

'Yes, it's all coming back,' said Rose. In fact it came back with a quick fast flood that she found painful. She remembered how the mother had looked when she appeared on television appealing about her son, and how untidy her hair had been; she remembered how the owner of the newspaper shop had managed to look both defensive and guilty when he was probably neither. She remembered the woman on the bus who was crying. Where *she* came in Rose had no idea but she clearly remembered the woman's tears. 'You didn't know him, did you, Steve?' Not specially known, not as a friend, surely she would have remembered.

'Yes, Steve did know him. They were in the same form.' Miss Fraser provided the answer. She looked at Mr Gordon, who spoke for the first time.

'I don't believe they were special friends. But I could be wrong.'

'Well, he didn't say anything to me.' But when did he ever say anything to her? Everyone, or almost everyone, had a secret life, but Steve's sometimes looked like a secret even from him.

'Inside the bag we found these . . .'

Jim Gordon unzipped the bag slowly, or it felt slowly to Rose, and took out, first a white sweater, then a light cotton shirt with matching trousers, the boys' sports outfit, and a crumpled tracksuit. She recognized them all as Steve's, they had his look somehow, smelt like him.

Then he held the bag out wide and let Rose look in. At the bottom of the bag, dented and crushed, looking as if they had been there undisturbed for some time were a pair of red boots. *The* red boots.

Rose raised her head from the survey. 'Ephraim's?'

She did not look at Steve, but she knew he was staring out of the window with the air of one who had nothing to do with what was going on here.

Now the policewoman came forward. 'I'm Joan Gilmour, Mrs Hilaire, Sergeant Joan Gilmour. These are the boots the boy was wearing when he disappeared. Or we think they are. We can't be quite sure without a positive identification from Mrs Humphreys. Or forensic proof. Or perhaps both... But Steve says he doesn't know anything about them.'

Rose shook her head. 'Then he doesn't.'

Gently the other woman said: 'From the look of it, they have been in his bag for some time... He must have seen them every time he went to the bag. But he won't say... We thought you might talk to him.'

Rose smiled, it was a game smile in the circumstances, but it stretched across her face like a grimace of pain. 'I don't believe Steve will talk to me. He doesn't usually. He might talk to me on the telephone, or he might write me a message, if he had something specific to say. Such as affected his own comfort, you understand...'

'Mrs Hilaire...' began Miss Fraser, her voice shocked, but Rose went on:

'He won't talk to me. If you want to get someone to talk to Steve then I suggest you try Miss Andrews who teaches English and drama. She likes him.'

'We all like Steve.'

Rose nodded. Good. So did she, she supposed, and a fat lot of good it did her. No, that wasn't true: she loved him, but she sometimes found it hard to like him.

'And Miss Andrews *has* spoken to Steve: she was there when the boots were found, as it happens.'

'This is serious, Mrs Hilaire,' said Sergeant Joan Gilmour. 'Can you make Steve see *how* serious and that we can't accept his story as it stands?'

'He knows it's serious, I expect.' She looked at her son. 'Well?'

Steve opened his mouth as if to speak.

'Be careful what you say, Steve,' said Jim Gordon.

Steve stopped talking even before he had started. Rose knew that phenomenon. It had started out in life with her and she still saw it daily, as if Steve had words ready to pour out to her and bit them back. She had stopped wondering why he did it. In her heart she knew that one day he would tell her and the truth would be hard to bear, better put it off.

A heavy silence settled on the room. Everyone in the room, except Rose, was wondering how to deal with it. The policewoman thought a good hard smack might be the answer, but couldn't be the one to deliver it. Jim Gordon knew he shouldn't have spoken and was regretting that he had opened his mouth; he was sunk in his own problem. So too for that matter was Lovella Fraser, who knew she had to control the situation and come out of it well; she knew, all the teachers at Hook Road School knew, that when the great amalgamation of three schools into one big comprehensive took place then the headship of that school would go to the best. She had to be the best. The rivalry among her peers was intense and so was the gossip about who was coping well with what.

They sat on for a while in silence. Steve obviously did not feel impelled to speak. Rose could have told them that at no time did he feel that obligation.

Lovella Fraser stood up. 'We can't leave the matter here, Steve, Mrs Hilaire, I'm sure you see that. The police will want to go on questioning you, Steve, and Sergeant Gilmour will probably have to take you down to the police station.'

—And you will be out of my hands and not under my direction to make you speak or not to speak. What she was doing was a failure of her responsibility to the boy, but a holding operation as regards her own career.

Sergeant Joan Gilmour got up too. 'Mrs Hilaire will have to come too. She must be there when we talk to her son.' Her voice was not friendly. Rose, an old inhabitant of Paradise Street, who had heard that tone from the police before, at once felt three feet tall and aged five, and someone who had stolen a bar of chocolate. Stolen it, as she now recalled, not because she had no money but because chocolate was rationed.

Rose stood up too, and as she did so brushed against the desk were the sports bag and its contents were laid out. The red boots slid to the floor.

Not one of them wanted to touch the boots, that was suddenly obvious.

And out of the boot rolled a small red object which moved a few feet across the floor with a funny little sideways motion like a crab.

Rose recognized it at once as a little spool such as was sometimes used in her factory to wind off surplus silk from the machines. A lot of pure silk thread was used, too expensive to waste. This was bright red silk like blood. One of Gabriel's designs had called for such silk. Rose knew it came from Belmodes, without another look.

It brought her factory right into the affair. Something would have to be done about it, although she wasn't sure what exactly.

Steve had been quicker than she; his foot had shot out and covered the spool. Their eyes met. He was almost going to say something to her.

'Raise your foot, Steve,' said the woman detective.

Rose took a deep breath. 'We'll come down to the station with you,' not removing her eyes from Steve's foot. 'I'll drive. I've got my car. We'll go together.'

It had got past denials and silence. She could see that even if Steve couldn't.

AFTER ALL, Coffin had had a happy couple of days; he had telephoned his house at midday and one of the workmen had answered. So he knew they were there, and might even be at work. It was even probable they were, since he had taken the precaution of asking his former landlady, now retired, Mrs Lorimer, to look in. She had a way with the idle.

Work, a dull but tricky investigation of an armed robbery, together with fraud and murder, had taken him out of his base all the afternoon, so that he almost missed an urgent personal telephone call. His work was undercover and it was best done discreetly. He was out of touch a good deal, that was policy. The whole area was experiencing a sharp uprise in crime, some small and petty, some violent, and Coffin was concerned about this. Another problem was drugs. A lot of hemp, a little heroin, and the new one to watch for, LSD 25, lysergic acid diethylamide, the hallucinatory drug, the so-called 'Vision of Hell' mixture.

He might have missed the call altogether if he hadn't dashed back to collect something; he had forgotten a lot of things lately and although it worried him he knew why: it was because he had one big thing he was remembering.

'Listen, you've got to know this.' It was Mary Lorimer speaking; she didn't announce herself which was unusual for her. 'They've found a dead body in your house.' The line went dead, again unlike Mrs Lorimer, who could usually be relied on for a good spell. It was a mark of her disturbance. Afterwards he discovered it was because she felt sick, having seen the remains.

It seemed the workmen had had a good day, Coffin's house warm and sunny. They inspected the roof first, then decided that the first task should be the floor in the kitchen. Coffin was having most of the floorboards replaced with good new wood. They started taking them up...

As Coffin walked down Mouncy Street, he saw a police car parked down the road. Outside his house. He started to hurry.

A body? In his house. His first house with a big mortgage still on it. Well, he would have to stay, he could not afford to move out. It was the first time he had had such a thoroughly unprofessional reaction to a corpse.

'I'm a first-time buyer,' he said to himself. 'I'm bound to feel bad.' It was not what he had expected in home-owning. He followed into the house a small, dark young woman, carrying a medical bag: he knew her to be the new Home Office forensic pathologist seconded to this Division.

He walked into the house. The front door opened into a small hall from which a small living-room opened to the right-hand side. Straight ahead was the old kitchen and behind the scullery. All these houses in Mouncy Street were the same.

THE FLOOR was up in the kitchen, but it was possible to tread across it by means of the underpinnings to the scullery, which was where everyone seemed to be.

The floor was up here too, but having been so rotten this was no surprise, nor was the stale smell in the air. He had smelt it every day since he had moved in and been told it was damp rot.

He went up to the door and looked down. They hadn't left it prone there for him to look at, they were waiting for the forensic team plus the photographers as he very well knew, but he felt a sense of possession about this poor sad object.

The two uniformed policemen both knew him, and nodded. 'Glad you got here. Been trying to get in touch.'

'I was out on a job.'

'Haven't seen you since the Wimpy Bar murder. Not around here, anyway.'

'Only just moved in. Well, not long anyway.'

'How long, John?'

'A few weeks.'

'Well, you're in luck there.'

They both moved over side by side and looked down the hole from a better point. The sunlight through the window showed how dark and stained the bundle was, bursting through its paper wrapping. It was unmistakably human, and yet... 'Been there some time,' said Coffin.

'I think so. Now, if you'd been living here for the last year...'

'You'd be asking me questions.' There was a grim humour in their interchange.

They still stared. Coffin spoke first.

'Small.' It was small.

'Might not be all there.'

'Cut up, you mean?'

'Well, in bits.'

Joints in wrapping? No, it was a complete thing in itself.

Coffin shook his head. 'That's not the way it looks to me.' He turned away. 'It's a whole thing, whatever it is.' He knew without realizing why that it was somehow worse than that.

As he walked away he understood why: he had seen a tiny, tiny little finger protruding from one end of the bundle.

It was a kid down there, a little shrivelled-up kid.

Once before in his professional life, early on when he was just starting out, Coffin had been involved with a child case. Well, there had been others, but that first one had been the marker. That first child had turned up safe, as it happened.

With a sigh, he could foretell all that was going to happen to him and his house now. They were going to be invaded. Uniformed policemen, plainclothes detectives, all together with forensic scientists and other laboratory workers would be made free of his house. The whole scene of the crime outfit would have a passport. As would the photographers, and possibly their partners if they could manage it. The only person who was likely to be kept out was John Coffin.

'The place has been empty for nearly two years,' he said thoughtfully. 'That's why I got it cheap.'

Now he knew what part of the price might be it did not come so cheap. But he still wanted to live in it. Everyone had to have a home and this was going to be his.

'Well, I'll just go outside and have a smoke.' There was a minute front garden with a red brick wall. He could sit on the wall in the sun and make a public spectacle of himself. 'Who's coming down, do you know?' He meant: which officer is going to head the investigation team? He knew most of the local men and had worked with some. With none was he specially friendly, they were a clannish lot around here.

'Jim Pedler, I think.'

He certainly knew Jim Pedler and had some respect for the Inspector. Or at any rate for his power of rising through the ranks. Whether he could see further into the wood than anyone else was another matter.

'He knows how to use a team,' he assessed.

'He's the boss,' said the young policeman. His tone said: And one I have to live with.

There was the sound of a car door banging and a brisk voice announced the arrival of Inspector Pedler and his associates. Coffin quietly withdrew.

As he had planned he sat on the wall in the sun and smoked a cigarette. He was experimenting with Turkish cigarettes, on the grounds that they represented a kind of luxury and he ought to know about luxury. He could not afford any other kind.

'I'll be around for a bit if you want me,' he said as he left the house. 'It's my evening class tonight.'

He got the baffled look of incomprehension he expected. This would have been intensified if he had said, not: Yes, it's woodwork; but: Actually, it's genealogy.

To take his mind off the small body in the house behind him, he thought about his genealogy class and his reason for taking it.

He had a good sound practical reason, or so he told himself, but it might have been self-deception, he might just have been indulging in a private fantasy.

Several years ago he had been searching for a long-lost sibling. About whom he had been told by an elderly relative. Another and younger child of his mother who had been put out to adoption. Or lost. Sometimes he thought deliberately lost. He had been on the hunt for his lost brother or sister. At one time he thought he had a good lead through a friendly butcher's, one of whom might have adopted this child. But that had come to nothing. He had gone on with the search to no purpose.

Now he had a new approach: he would dig back into the family history and see if something emerged that way. To teach him how to do this basic research he was attending classes on the subject at the local Adult Education Centre on Charlton Hill. Mrs Lorimer believed his real reason was that he fancied the class teacher.

He did like the girl, it must be admitted, but his heart was still locked in a love-affair of long ago. Long to him, that is, a matter of six years, although when he worked on his genealogy it counted as but yesterday.

As he sat there smoking, he looked down the road to where the Belmodes factory was just visible. Old inhabitants, of whom he was beginning to know a few, had told him that before it was Belmodes making clothes, it was a furniture factory that did not survive the war.

One cigarette and then another. He took a stroll up the road and then back again, vaguely seeking entertainment. He could have thought about the case he was working on, but there had been three fruitless days on that and he wanted a change. He could have thought about his evening class, but even that did not attract at the moment.

The working day was over at Belmodes, but there were still women about, popping in and out of the shops. He was bound to say that they looked cheerful and not toilworn. Whatever it was, Belmodes was clearly not a sweatshop. A small crowd of onlookers was standing to stare curiously at his house with the sinister activity within. Somehow, they knew there was a body found.

Walking on her own was a girl he recognized. He had seen her only that morning at the bus stop where he changed buses. As a matter of fact he saw her every morning. She was an exceedingly pretty girl and she wore the short skirts he liked. So this was where she came.

He stood up, not without the hope of attracting her attention. As she drew level their eyes met. She looked first surprised, then pleased.

'Hello.'

'Hello.'

Gabriel blushed. 'I've seen you at the bus stop.'

'I know. I remember.'

'Did you notice? I didn't know... Do you live here?'

'More or less,' said Coffin grimly.

Gabriel's gaze flickered to the police car. 'Is there something wrong?'

'I'm not sure.'

She accepted the cautious reply for the dubious currency it was. A childhood in Paradise Street had accustomed her to both police cars and evasive replies.

'The police is the police.' She had her portfolio of photographed designs under her arm; she was already experiencing the first feelings of guilt about what she was doing to Rose. She gave Coffin a wave, then walked on. 'One of them behind you wants you,' she said over her shoulder.

The uniformed man walked down the path to John Coffin and sat down on the wall.

'You're in luck.'

'Glad to hear it.'

'The body's only half yours. You share it with next door. The whole parcel is part under your floor, and part under next door. Looks as though it may have gone in that way.'

'That house is lived in.'

'A year ago it wasn't.'

'A year ago, eh? As long as that?'

'The lady doc says so. And it's upset her. A boy it is, young kid. And so she thought it might be the Humphreys boy. His red boots have turned up locally, so it all fitted in. But no: this one's been in too long.'

And yet Coffin had thought it might be even longer. The dried-up-looking parcel he had seen had looked as if more years than one had browned it. Done it to a turn.

'Apparently there's something in the soil round here that dries out tissue but also darkens. Too much of something or the other, the doc says.' His tone was respectful.

Dr Mary MacMiller was a newcomer, but one to be handled carefully; she had a sharp way with those who presumed on her sex and good looks.

'Clue to identity?'

The other policeman shook his head.

'So now it's Who, When, How?'

'The usual three.'

'Well, it's your case,' said Coffin cheerfully. 'And not mine. I only live here.'

TWO

WHEN Gabriel saw the women workers going into Belmodes in the mornings, she marvelled at the work they turned out. In a time of full employment such as they were enjoying, Rose Hilaire had had to take what workers she could get. What she got were a few young girls and a group of middle-aged women coming back to work after years of running a home. The miracle was that Rose had welded them into a team, and one with a sense of responsibility as well as high standards. Looking at them as they streamed in and stamped their time cards and took off nylon headscarfs and tweed coats, she could hardly believe the delicacy and precision of the work they would presently produce. When she sat in the rest-room and watched them eat their sandwiches (Rose was planning a canteen, but had not built it yet), she was always pleasantly surprised that no crumbs and grease got on to the delicate fabrics. But they never did.

'Gabriel—can I tell you something?'

She took a long drink of hot black coffee and swallowed two aspirins. She had a bad headache and a worse case of bad conscience. A restless night's sleep had not eased her mind at all. She had a small art room at Belmodes where she was meant to design, but in fact she wandered around restlessly when ideas ran short. She was at present in the rest-room.

'What is it, Shirley?'

Shirley was one of Rose's best workers; she could cut a pattern like an angel, and get more dresses out of a given length of material than you would think possible. Rose, no mean exponent of that art, had trained her herself.

Shirley had been born around the corner from Paradise Street but was busy easing herself out of its influence. She was ambitious. If Gabriel eyed Rose enviously, then Shirley was probably eyeing Gabriel. As far as Gabriel could see, she had enormous talent and style, but had had no formal training in design. This might or might not matter, Gabriel was still marking time on this one. The two young women usually eyed each other warily.

'It's about Steve...well, and what happened yesterday. Should we say anything to Rose? You know, say how sorry we are. Or should we say nothing? You know her better than we do.'

The whole muttered conversation in the workrooms that morning had been about the body found in Mouncy Street and the connection of the dead body with Steve Hilaire.

Everyone knew how he had been taken down to the police station with his mother late yesterday afternoon. They also knew he had come back.

'Not sure about that.' Gabriel hesitated. 'Don't know.'

'Yes, you do,' persisted Shirley. 'You work with her more. And we want to get it right. Do we say something or not?'

Rumours had been flying around the workrooms all the morning, varying in intensity and accuracy with the character of the speaker. Rose was mostly liked and respected as an employer, but inevitably she had her critics. One of these, a stockroom assistant called Ted Tipper who had clashed more than once with Rose on union matters, had said that he had heard that Rose herself had been questioned about the finding of the red boots in Steve's sports bag. The general reaction was that perhaps she had, perhaps she hadn't. Ted was a man working in a factory run by women for women and he appeared to resent it. He had a harried existence.

'Ask Dagmar.' If anyone was close to Rose, it was Dagmar.

'You know she won't talk. It's a fact of life that Dagmar will not talk about Rose. Whether that means she loves her or hates her, I've never felt sure.'

Gabriel ignored that comment. In her opinion Dagmar Blond had total loyalty to her employer and love did not come into it. The roots were probably economic and historical.

'Well, Steve's back. He's gone to school, as far as you know. It's a nothing; I should ignore it.'

'But they've found a dead body. And not far away from here.'

'Not the body of the boy who is missing, though. Not the boy from Hook Road School. I mean, the body that's been found had nothing to do with Steve or Rose.'

As far as Gabriel saw it, that was how that matter rested, but she could see that the workrooms couldn't leave it there. They enjoyed the idea, whether they would admit it or not, that their employer might be mixed up with murder. It gave them a thrill. Murder of a child was the English crime.

'I don't see Rose as a child murderer.'

'I'm not saying so. Of course not. None of us would say that. But she came into work with red eyes. She'd been crying.'

Gabriel shrugged. 'Leave it.'

'I don't think we can. The boy that is missing, the one with the red boots, is nephew to Lily Bates.'

Lily Bates was one of the older members of the sewing-room; she had worked in Bianca Mosca's salon as an apprentice before her marriage and was much respected by her fellows.

Gabriel looked down at her hands.

'I didn't know that.'

'You don't know everything on the shop floor. Anyway, Lily's been away sick. But she's back today. We have to say something to Rose.'

'I suppose what you are saying is that if I don't, then Lily will.'

'She's come back to say something. Have you seen her?'

Gabriel hesitated. 'You don't mean she'd attack Rose?'

Shirley gave a shrug. 'If she thinks Rose or her son know anything about her nephew, then I think she'd tear them apart to find out.'

'The police can't think so.' If they had then they'd have hung on to Steve. Of course, he was only a kid, but still . . .

From the door Dagmar said: 'Thought I'd find you two here.' She made it an accusation. 'Mrs Hilaire wants you, Shirley . . . And Gaby, we can't match the trimmings for the blue chiffon shirt dress, not at our price . . . Rose says it's up to you.'

She let the door fall with a bang. No other comment was needed.

Shirley was without rancour: 'She heard all that. She'll go straight to Rose.'

'Save us, then!'

Gaby opened the rest-room door and, still clutching her mug of coffee, sped off down the passage to the stockrooms; she knew from experience that the discord usually started there. Even when she had gone to considerable trouble to find trimmings that were right and at the agreed price, they usually got it wrong. Like all well-trained recruits from Paradise Street, she suspected graft somewhere. Probably someone's cousins somewhere had a factory that... She never had to finish the sentence, but ended with the word money.

As she sped along she did not miss the air of suppressed excitement everywhere. So they did really believe that Steve Hilaire was in trouble. Nasty.

Ted Tipper hurried through the corridors, he felt the atmosphere and did not enjoy it. A whole workforce of women alarmed him anyway. He passed Gabriel warily, she was not one of those he specially feared, but you had to be careful. He went into the cubbyhole he had built for himself out of packing boxes so that he could swallow an indigestion tablet in privacy. No one had any idea of the pressures a man could be under.

Gabriel had a rapid and scorching interview with Theda, the head of the stockroom, then turned into her art-room. She was immediately aware that there was someone there: Sitting in her only chair, and staring out of the window.

'Lily!' The last person she had expected in her room, where hardly anyone came. Dagmar penetrated occasionally and so did Shirley. Rose rarely. She summoned you when she wanted you, a pattern of behaviour that Gabriel meant to emulate in her turn one day.

'Lily, what is it? Do you want me?'

Lily did not move, she hardly looked at Gabriel. 'No. This is the only quiet place I could find to be on my own. And I wanted a rest.'

'You don't look well.'

And it was true. Lily, who never looked robust, was pinched and frail with a blue mark like a bruise on each cheekbone beneath the eyes.

'I've just had a bit of bad news.'

'Oh Lily, what?' Gabriel drew up the only other chair and sat down beside her.

Musingly, almost to herself, Lily said: 'Gave it to myself, you might say.'

Gabriel sat quiet.

'You know what I'm talking about?'

'Sort of.' Gabriel bent her head. 'Your nephew.'

'Yes... Been gone for weeks. Dear little chap. Always small for his age, but wiry. Called me Aunty Billy for Best-loved Aunt Lily.' Then she said, 'You heard about his boots?'

'Yes.' What else was there to say?

'I've been away ill... Not so much ill as upset. Not mental.'

'Of course not.'

'Nothing like that. Doctors said I should have a rest from work. Put me on Valium. Ever had it?'

Gabriel shook her head.

'I knew I'd got to come back when I heard last night about Steve having the boots...and that other little boy's body.'

'I didn't know it was a boy, that wasn't in the papers. Are you sure you aren't jumping to conclusions?'

'The policeman that lives in the house is a friend of a neighbour, he let him know.'

'Good lord, that's what he is: he's a policeman.' Gabriel had wondered what John Coffin worked at and now she knew.

'Yes... A little lad, it was. Been there some time.'

'Well, then it's not your nephew.'

'The police think he might be another one. One in a row.'

It was possible. If there was one murdered boy there might be another. But at the moment the connection must be mostly in the mind, although she could understand how Lily's imagination must seize upon it. Unless the police had some hard information making a connection that Coffin had not passed on to Lily's friend. That was possible too.

'That's just pub talk.'

'No, I found something.' She dropped the statement into the conversation like a lead weight.

Gabriel felt it hit her.

'What did you find?'

'I'll show you.' But Lily stayed still without moving. 'Know the rest-room?'

'Of course.'

'Know the little cupboard under the washbasins?'

'I know what you mean.' She had never investigated it. As far as she knew, clean paper towels, fresh soap and rolls of lavatory paper were kept in it.

Gabriel followed Lily down the corridor. There was one solitary woman standing staring at her face in the mirror over the washbasins.

'My poor face,' she said without looking at them. 'Disaster.' Then she put some more lipstick on, a pale intense colour with a lot of blue in it, and walked out, still without looking at them.

Lily had behaved as if she was not there. Nor did she act as if she saw anyone else; Gabriel began to feel she was not there either.

Lily advanced towards the cupboards and pulled open the door. 'Take no notice of her, she's never had any time for herself since her husband left her.'

'I didn't think you noticed her.'

'She's always in here.' Lily was digging away in the back of the cupboard. She sat back on her heels, digging away like a little animal. 'What upsets her is he didn't leave her for anyone else . . . He moved out to a place in Wapping and is growing his hair long and wearing a white smock, I saw him the other day when he came back to get some money out of her.' A roll of lavatory paper arrived at Gabriel's feet. 'Here. Look... I didn't touch it, I wanted a witness.'

So that's what I am, thought Gabriel, I'm a witness.

'You'll have to get down.'

Gabriel obligingly crouched on her knees to look inside the cupboard.

'Right at the back...'

Nervously Gabriel put her head in the cupboard, wondering what she was going to find. Nothing dead?

'I found it when I was looking for fresh soap.'

Not true, thought Gabriel at once, you were looking.

At the back of the cupboard she saw a small bundle of crumpled cloth. It had once been white but was now discoloured. Nor did she believe that Lily had left it untouched. To her it looked as though it had been screwed up in a tighter ball: you could see the stained folds.

'So what is it?'

Lily hardly bothered to hide that she had had a closer look. "I think it's Ephraim's pants. His cotton underpants.'

'Oh, Lily, you can't know. Just an old rag used for cleaning the floor.'

'Rubbish. I'm going to get it out. You watch, and remember what you see.'

She drew out the bundle, and slowly opened it out. It might once have been a boy's underpants, or part of them. It was no longer a complete anything. And very stained with some dark stuff.

'It's a rag, just a rag.' Gabriel looked at Lily. 'Truly, it could be anything. Just a bit of cloth for cleaning the floor.'

She knew she wasn't going to carry conviction, she read the determination on Lily's face.

'No, it's his, and that's blood.' Lily pointed to the stains, blotchy and thunderous. 'Blood that someone has tried to wash out and failed.'

'I don't know.'

'And look at the bottom of the cupboard.'

'Yes,' said Gabriel thoughtfully. Where the bundle had rested was an area of stained board that seemed to take its shape from what had sat on it. In an uncertain voice, she said, 'If you're really worried you'd better tell the police.'

Lily gave her a brilliant smile. 'Something else to do first.'

ROSE WAS SITTING at her desk. She had been crying, the gossips were quite right, the shock of what had happened to her had been considerable. She did not know why her son had the other lad's red boots in his sports bag, but she accepted his story that he had not put them there. Hard, though, to believe there was not more to the story than he was telling. She could sense trouble hanging over him. He was not telling everything. No doubt the police felt the same way, but they had kept his bag and let Steve himself depart.

When they got home he had gone straight up to his room and closed the door. She heard the lock turn. No more talking between them.

Later she carried up a tray of food and knocked on his door. 'I've brought your supper, Steve... Made your favourite scrambled eggs on fried bread. Then some apple tart with cream.' One constant had remained between them until now: she had known what he liked to eat and had laboured to produce it. 'Come on now, open up. You know you must be hungry.'

Silence and silence again. Perhaps if we had a telephone each we could talk, she thought with a bitter humour.

In the end she left the tray outside his room and went to bed. It was gone in the morning and the plate and knife and fork washed up and put away.

While she was standing by the kitchen sink with a cup of black coffee, Steve came down the stairs dressed for school.

'Don't go to school.' It wasn't going to be easy for him. 'Have the day at home. I'll write a note or telephone... You can go tomorrow.' Or even later; a week might not be too long to hide.

He shook his head, walked past her and out of the door. He was going to be very, very early for morning school, but apparently even that was better than staying in the house with her.

She put the coffee down and began to get herself ready for work, checking her make-up and patting her pocket for the car keys. Not there. Well, she'd had them last night so they couldn't be far, but the spare keys hung on the rack in the kitchen and she could take those.

The spare keys were there all right, but not where she kept them. She was methodical about where different keys hung, priding herself on the routine. Now the spare car keys were hung on the top of a set of house keys. Carelessly, casually.

The act had Steve's signature all over it, almost as if he wanted her to see and know what he had done. What had he done? Had he taken the keys and played around with her car?

She replaced the keys where they should go. One of those nights, she thought, when I took a sleeping tablet. No, not the night, doesn't even have to be the night. Early morning would do. No one around. Perhaps this very morning.

With tears pouring down her cheeks and shaking with misery and rage, she found her handbag and the other car keys. At least they were where she had left them.

She went back to her mug of coffee and stood at the sink, crying and drinking. The coffee was no longer hot, it wouldn't do her any good. She needed to be done good to, she knew that they were both in terrible trouble.

Ever since he had been born she had loved her son. But apparently she had not been very good at showing it or he would have loved her back, which he could not do. Not and behave the way he did to her.

She did not look at her morning paper nor listen to the radio as she drove to work, so she did not learn the news about the body in Mouncy Street. Afterwards she realized that Steve could not have known either when he set out. Poor kid, poor kid. What had he walked into? What had she, for that matter?

She knew the police would be into the factory: there was that matter of the silk. That put Belmodes right in the picture. She was surprised that the police had let them both go home. It had a just-for-the-time-being feel to it.

And then she had her own particular worry. Surely at her age she couldn't be in the club again? She'd been so careful. God, if she escaped this time, she'd go on the Pill, in spite of the headaches. She knew a useful quack who would give her a prescription.

'It was the night I tried cannabis.' In the fashion world it was difficult to avoid cannabis at the moment without feeling you had got left behind. Rose never liked to get left behind.

She hung up her short lime-green linen coat and replenished her lipstick. It was pale, pale pink, very nearly the whitest shade of white, but all that fashion allowed at the moment. Nor did she wear powder and rouge, the shiny, natural face being required, although her eyelashes were false and long.

The tresses of blonde hair curling down her back were false too, her own hair would not grow beyond her shoulders. As a result, she envied Gabriel her shining mane and had more than once been tempted to give it a tug to see if it was artificial also.

She had met no one on her way in, but already, in a mad kind of way, she felt like Myra Hindley. Something bad had touched her and Steve and discoloured them.

She sat down at her desk to start work. It was necessary to consider her programme for the next two seasons. She knew how much she depended on Gabriel's flair and taste. For years she had succeeded by quietly pilfering ideas from Paris or Rome. Now London was leading the way. Marvellous, good for trade. But it also meant you had to have some ideas of your own. Gabriel had the ideas.

Rose surveyed a portfolio of drawings; each was colour-matched in swatches of silk, wool and cotton. Gabriel was suggesting combinations of trousers and short tunics. Were her ideas too extreme? There had to be a certain element of hot pants, fashion was going that way, but Rose's market demanded tact.

From outside she could hear Dagmar's voice. One day she might escape from Dagmar, but at the moment they seemed firmly stuck together by their past. She could never decide whether Dagmar liked her or really disliked her. She had grown up with Dagmar and never known.

There was another voice mixing with Dagmar's now and they were both raised.

She got up and went to the door. 'What is this— Lily, I thought you were ill?' She remembered then about Lily's missing nephew.

She sounded nastier than she meant, but all the same she was surprised at what she got back.

'You shut up and listen to me.'

'Lily...'

Lily did look ill. Or rather, strange. As she looked at Lily's face she saw in it a reflection of what must be in her own that morning: the pain, the anger, and yes, the alienation. They had both looked at something unspeakable: they were different from other people now.

'What have you and that bastard done to my nephew?'

'I don't know what you mean.'

'You've had him here; I've found the traces. Where is he now?'

Lily took an aggressive step forward. Dagmar got between them.

'Don't be silly, you're beside yourself, Lily. Mrs Hilaire doesn't know anything about your nephew.'

'Look at her face, and you can see she does. We all know what was found where.'

Lily stood there, small, stocky and raging. 'If you've hurt my Ephraim I'll kill you,' she said to Rose. 'Gabriel, go and telephone the police; I'm going back to guard what I found. Remember: you're my witness.'

Gabriel looked across to Rose; the message that passed between them frightened Gabriel with its starkness.

Suddenly, she believed in murder. It wasn't hypothetical, or jokey, or something that happened to other people. Not foreign territory at all. Murder was for anyone.

AFTER THE POLICE in the person of a detective-constable had arrived, inspected Lily's find, and taken it away, sealing the cupboard and saying tests would be made, Gabriel was not surprised to get a summons to Rose Hilaire's office.

She had been expecting it. In the corridor she passed Dagmar, who was complaining bitterly that all supplies of lavatory paper and sanitary towels had been locked away. As Gabriel walked on she heard Ted Tipper being detailed to bring in fresh supplies. He looked as though he wanted to run away.

Gabriel felt the same: she could guess at the coming interview with Rose.

'Somehow she knows,' she reported to Charley that evening, when they were drinking coffee in his flat. 'She knows a lot too much. All of it. I had a lousy day.'

She had emerged from Rose's office with Rose still shouting at her, while the whole shop floor had heard her shouting back. After that it had not been an easy day's work with an excited workroom and a hostile Dagmar.

'I'll kill her,' Gabriel said simply to Charley, 'if she grabs that set of designs, and she means to. I've put my heart into them, and they are mine. I haven't stinted her in what I've done for Belmodes, but these are special, the best I've got in me.'

Charley looked at her with silent sympathy; he thought he knew as much as she did about putting your heart in.

'I like Rose Hilaire,' Gaby was almost in tears. 'She's a great woman in her way, and I see she's got problems, but she makes me mad.'

'I hear rumours going around,' said Charley. 'What did she say about that?'

Gabriel shrugged. 'We didn't discuss it. But she's sending on messages all the same.' And fierce angry ones they were as well.

'Saying what?'

'She's frightened, of course.'

Charley's living-room in Mouncy Street was also his studio. From the wall the figure of the woman who sold hot potatoes underneath the railway arch stared out at the room from the several hats (she always wore two) and shawls that wrapped her. Hanging next was a glittering photograph of Nancy Woolright, last year's Beauty Queen of London. Next to her was a shot, apparently spontaneous, a flick of the shutter, of a street scene at Greenwich market with a trio of boys at a bookstall. There were plenty of others, townscapes, portraits, even some of his best fashion photographs, but Gabriel was so used to them she hardly saw them, not noticing that Charley changed them at intervals.

What he did not change was the rest of the décor: the old worktable, the even older chairs, and the lighting equipment suspended ready for use.

Charley did not count among Gabriel's list of attractive men; she had known him such a long time that he was unsexed. Nothing more than a friendly kiss even passed between them, for which Charley was grateful.

He knew his Gabriel, give her an inch and she took a mile, he had no desire to wake up and find himself in bed beside her.

'I've met a lovely policeman,' said Gabriel.

JOHN COFFIN, happily unaware how his name had been on both Lily and Gabriel's lips, was engaged in his homework. On a tray in front of him was his supper, and by his side on the table the book he was studying on how to trace your ancestors. He was reading the chapter on Parish Records while he ate baked beans with sausages.

His colleagues who were investigating the body found under the floorboards had let him have his living-room back but the kitchen was still barred.

His telephone rang. 'Yes.' He was far away in 1837 when the registration of births, deaths and marriages was made compulsory. Before that you had to go to parish registers. Coffin had been startled to learn Thomas Cromwell had been responsible for instigating them.

A local policeman, an old friend, was on the phone.

'We've got an ID on the body,' said Philip Jordan.

'Who?'

'A lad from Essex. Eddie Jackson: 12 Archer Avenue, Hornchurch. He was aged thirteen and had run away several times, so he was not reported missing as soon as he might have been. Family thought he'd come back.'

'So he has got a family?'

'When I say family, they weren't what you'd call close, he had a grandmother and a stepfather, and of the two I'd say the stepfather cared for him most.'

'Mother dead?'

'Gone off. No one knows where. Not dead, though, as she sends the odd postcard. The natural father has remarried and lives in Canada.'

'So no one really cared if he was around or not?'

Coffin thought: Poor kid.

'I wouldn't say that: I think the stepfather does mind, but he isn't the brightest fellow in the world. As for the grandmother, she's a bit past it. Hardly knows the time of day.'

'Why did he run away the first time? Anything special?'

'Yes, it was in a way. He had a liking for one of his schoolteachers who moved to another area and tried to find him.'

'And did he?'

'No. Didn't have any luck, the chap had left London. Then he just drifted around till he was picked up.

Went off again after that, but came back under his own steam. The third time, not.'

'And then he turns up in Mouncy Street.' Coffin added, 'And not too far away the boots of another missing boy turned up in school. Worth thinking about it, isn't it?'

'Something more on Ephraim. What looks like a piece of boy's underpants was found in a cupboard in Belmodes.'

'Belmodes? That Rose Hilaire's outfit?' And workplace of the gorgeous Gabriel of the longest hair and the shortest skirts.

'That's right. There are also stains—in the cupboard, and on the fabric, could be blood.'

'And is it?'

Cautiously his informant said, 'It appears to be human blood. Can't go any further at the moment, could be the boy's.'

The scientists had another task also. The whole of the cupboard in which the stained clothes had been found had been removed to the laboratory. The blood was blood group A. It was the group of Ephraim Humphreys. Also the blood group of forty per cent of the population.

'Thanks for telling me.' Coffin thought he would now go back to his family. After all, it wasn't his case.

But he was still a bit curious.

'Anything else to say?'

'Know who used to live in your house before you?'

'No. It was empty for over a year.' The row of modest houses had fallen into disfavour as old-fashioned and beyond change, but now as house prices rose higher, people were moving back in.

'Old man Mossycop. Last tenant.'

'Good Lord! I had no idea he went on so long.'

Coffin sat thinking about it. Fancy old Mossycop having lived in what was now his house. He was a figure from the past all right. Mossycop, a nickname for Edward Mosse, had been a well-known local figure. A tram-driver before the war, he had come into his own as an Auxiliary Fireman with AFS proudly emblazoned on the shoulder of his uniform. People said he loved that uniform more than his wife and certainly he looked after it better. He had stayed on in the Fire Service as long as the war had lasted and kept the uniform even after.

As well as his fire-fighting, Edward Mosse had helped to run a Boys' Club. A lot of lads like John Coffin had been members pre-war, before the evacuation and then the call-up drew them away.

'I had no idea he went on so long,' he repeated.

'Hardly did. He got pretty senile towards the end. Died at home, though, and don't we all want to do that?' There was an odd note in his informant's voice.

'What else? There is something.'

Again that odd note. 'You wouldn't have noticed when you took a look-in. No way of seeing. But when the boy's body was moved, there was another one underneath.'

'Another boy?'

'No. It looks like it was Mossycop. Think of that.'

THREE

ROSE was up against it.

Blood in her factory; another body found, and possibly identified. (The news had spread around in spite of police silence. No true blue inhabitant of Paradise Street or Mouncy Street ever needed to be told anything from the police; they had ways of finding out.)

Rose put on more make-up and let her workers know it was business as usual. Under her firm gaze they bent to their machines. She had given Lily a holiday with pay, but Lily had obstinately reappeared and was working with the rest. Her face looked puffy.

There was a truce between Rose and Gabriel, but none between Shirley and Gabriel because Gaby had discovered it to be Shirley who had leaked her secret to Rose. She had been searching Gaby's workroom, but she must have had her suspicions before. I suppose I'm easily read, thought Gabriel. In future she would be more careful. Discovery did not alter her plans, only slowed them down.

Dagmar Blond moved about the factory as an unfriendly, enigmatic figure. This was the face that Paradise Street turned on outsiders.

Steve had gone back to school, where he kept his head down and avoided his enemies; he felt as if the whole school was his enemy.

Where Ephraim was no one knew.

Rose shut herself into her office, grimly applying herself to routine. She was expecting another visit from the police. And not about what had been found in the factory.

There was something else. She knew it. Dagmar knew it too, she could see it in her eyes.

They would have to talk it over.

John Coffin, on his way to work, stopped at the delicatessen to buy one of their warm ham rolls, then took it into Cat's Coffee Shop to eat with a cup of the best Kenya. He still had no kitchen.

Cat was presiding in person behind the counter. A keen follower of fashions, he had been a notable Ted in his day, but had now abandoned the narrow trousers and sharp haircut in favour of golden locks curling on his shoulders worn with a loose striped robe bought in Egypt. He had retained his grandpa's Albert, however, and wore the watch and chain looped round his neck like a medallion.

At a table in the corner Coffin saw his friend, Philip Jordan, communicator of the news about Mossycop.

'Hello, Phil. What are you doing here? Coffee, please, Cat.'

'Having breakfast, then going to Mouncy Street.'

Cat came across with the coffee, casting a disapproving glance at Coffin's ham roll. 'I could have done you one of those.'

'I wanted one without you smoking hash all over it.'

'I *never*.' But there was no anger in Cat's voice; his bright, clear eyes were focusing in the distance, seeing eternal Peace and Joy.

'One bob. Peace, friend,' he said, while sweeping the money into his pocket. 'Peace and Joy.'

'So it was old Mossycop?' Coffin stirred his coffee. All night he had been thinking: I've been sleeping over Mosse's dead body.

'Looks like it.' Jordan drank his coffee down to the bottom. 'Eddie Davis was on the job. He looked down in the hole and he saw Mossycop in his uniform. You know he always wore it for gardening. "My God," he said. "It looks like Mossycop down there."'

'So who was it buried before, if it wasn't Mosse?'

'Ask someone else. And guess who it was made the original identification and said, "Yes, that's Uncle Mosse" and was his sole heir?'

'Well, who?'

'Rose Hilaire.'

Whichever way you looked at it, that name seemed to come up at every term: Rose Hilaire mother of Steve, employer of Lily, and niece of a body under Coffin's floorboards.

'Do you know her?'

'No.' He must have bought his house off her, remotely. There had been another name: Lee.

They passed out of the shop together, side by side, falling automatically into step.

Cat watched them go, all about him hung a sweet smoky smell.

'We'll raid you one day, Cat. So watch it,' called Jordan companionably over his shoulder.

Cat called after them, 'I can take criticism. But leave me my love-life.'

'What's he mean?' Coffin asked.

Jordan shrugged. 'They call his place Shrew's Corner.'

'Why shrew?'

'Small, supple creatures with sharp teeth—that's the sort he likes.'

Coffin grunted. Yes, that was Cat's way of life: he would always be the sex that seemed fashionable at the time.

At the bus stop he looked hopefully for Gabriel. No sign. Wonder where she is, he thought.

GABRIEL WAS SITTING by Rose's side in the Porsche. Rose drove slowly, but her face was stiff with tension. Out of the corner of her eye she was watching Gabriel.

She slowed down at the traffic lights by Sloane Street. The two women were on an inspection tour of the Rose Hilaire empire: Baker Street, Bond Street, Knightsbridge and Sloane Street. In spite of all her problems Rose was keeping to schedule.

Baker Street had been inspected and its records checked. No one fingered the till in Rose's jurisdiction. Bond Street had been looked over and found wanting: the clothes not displayed as they should be, the new vendeuse lacking in charm.

'It's the wrong end of Bond Street,' grumbled Rose. (Why hadn't the police been to see her? She would feel so much happier if they had and it was over. She had rehearsed what she would say.) 'It's getting too much like Carnaby Street, that patch.' She avoided a car trying to turn right where it should not, and turned left. Her Sloane Street shop was between an antique shop and a florist's. She had got the lease two years ago in 1964.

'I'm thinking of the Fulham Road. It's coming up fast.' She parked the car. 'If Belmodes survives. Sometimes I think it'll all end up Biba.'

Sometimes Gabriel thought the same herself. She slumped lower in her seat and kept quiet.

'What chance have I got with little cows like you short-changing me?'

'Haven't done anything yet,' muttered Gabriel.

'And nor will you. I've fixed it with Teddy Touch. I felt like leaving you to him. You almost deserve it, but not quite. No one deserves Teddy Touch.' She turned in her seat to stare at Gabriel grimly. 'You don't know the rules of this dirty game yet, though you think you do. One day I'll teach you how to go about ditching your contract.' She opened the car door and swung her long, beautiful legs out. She was one of those whom tights, as opposed to stockings, suited. She had better legs than Gabriel, and knew it. Her tights were pale, pale, a whiter shade of pale, only women with perfect legs can wear that shade. 'Oh no, darling, you didn't think you were the first clever little bitch to have the idea? It's been tried before, love, and better. It's the law of the jungle, kid, and you'd better know it.'

'All right.' Gabriel got out of the car and side by side they walked into Belmodes, Sloane Street, in bad-tempered silence.

Once inside the shop, however, acrimony faded; they were so alike that it was impossible for them to work together and be at odds.

Gabriel saw at once that a bell-shaped shift of her own design was being wrongly displayed, while Rose saw to her fury that a whole line of trousers and tabards had been wrongly priced. The errors in both cases were minute, but the experts were angered. They advanced to attack.

But before they could start in, Rose was called to the telephone.

'A call from the factory, Mrs Hilaire,'' said the shop manager. 'They said it's important. Asked you to ring back.' She too had heard the rumours, the telephones from shop to shop must have been red hot, and she looked at Rose with speculation.

Gabriel sat down in a chair to wait, her gaze moving round the shop. Rose had chosen to have all her shops decorated in apricot and green with clear white paint; it looked stylish and fresh. In the background the latest Beatles' success was humming away. Rose had decreed there should be music in her shops, and she had selected the repertoire herself. It was changed every two months, making it an expensive item, but one Rose thought essential, as setting the character for an Hilaire shop.

This particular jewel in the Hilaire crown looked in need of repolishing, however. To Gabriel's eye, there was a slight but perceptible air of neglect, due probably to a slack manager. The tall girl who had despatched Rose to the telephone was now studying her face in the wall mirror.

Rose emerged from the back room with a swirl of skirts. Her face was flushed, but her mouth set in a firm line.

'Gaby, we're off. I'm wanted down there.' Over her shoulder she said, 'Flavia, I shall be back. I'm not

happy with the look of things here. You've let it go.
Pull it up or you're out.'

As they drove off with some fast acceleration, Rose
said, 'She's probably out, anyway. I've had my eye on
her. Stupid cow, she thinks I don't know what goes on.
Her boyfriend has taught her to drink. Worse, too, I
expect. No, she'll have to go.'

Gabriel kept quiet, well aware she was not Rose's
favourite girl either. She would have liked to ask what
was up, but questions were not invited.

'Right here,' she said seeing that Rose seemed to be
about to drive on, unthinking.

Rose turned right, and seemed to relax a little. Being Rose, this gave her energy to devote to Gabriel.

'That Charley: he's a good photographer.'

So Rose not only knew, but had *seen*; somehow she
had got hold of Charley's photographs. That needed
thinking about.

'He's clever.' He was more than that, but hard to say
what. Inside, Charley was hard to gauge.

Rose laughed. 'You're surprised? You're like that
girl Flavia: you think I don't know what goes on
around me, but I've got my eyes open.'

Shirley's eyes, too, no doubt.

'Do you live with him?'

'No. Not in that way. Sometimes he stays around,
but it's only a matter of convenience when we're
working. If it's any business of yours.'

'None, of course. But you're jealous of him.'

'I might be,' muttered Gabriel, stung.

She was jealous. Charley did not make love to her, and he ought. She felt very strongly that he ought to want to. She might say no, but he ought to try. Her conclusion was that there was someone else.

But she'd never seen that someone. It was tough being jealous of a nobody.

Rose gave a laugh. 'You kid, you've got a lot to learn.'

'I'll learn it.'

'We all think that,' said Rose. 'But somehow you never learn quite enough. Take it from me.' She drove for a few minutes in silence, then she said, 'You know what I'm going back to?'

'I can guess. The police want to see you.'

'I've been expecting it ever since I heard that they found Uncle Mosse underneath the floorboards. I can't believe it.' She shook her head. 'How could he be there? He's dead and buried.'

'Perhaps someone dug him up.'

'Oh, funny. Listen, I'm going to tell you this and you can believe it or not: Uncle Mosse had been dead about a week when they took me in to identify him. He could have been anyone but he was in the right place: on his own bed in his own house in Mouncy Street, so it had to be him. Only now it looks as if it wasn't.'

Rose sounded angry, exasperated with life for arranging things so badly.

'Not his fault,' said Gabriel in a placatory way. Trying in spite of herself to be a peacemaker.

'I hadn't seen him for six years anyway. He hated the sight of me. There's no one he'd have wanted seeing him dead less than me, and the feeling was mutual. But by then there was only him and me left.'

'And your son.'

'Steve? I kept him away from the old man. They weren't good for each other.'

Rose said it as if she did not realize what a strange but interesting thing she had said. Gabriel did realize.

If I knew that policeman better, the one I met at the bus stop, she thought, I'd be tempted to tell him, because it tells you how Rose felt about her son. She fears him.

Not that it would help the policeman understand Steve. Rose had a problem there. Manipulative, that boy. She thought anyone who loved Steve would be getting a very poor bargain indeed. But then, in matters of love and war, it is *caveat emptor*: Let the buyer watch out.

She could see behind Rose's phrase a fear that Steve might indeed know something about the bodies.

It was a nasty picture of family life.

Gabriel herself had not had a happy family life, but a merciful providence, as she now saw it, had orphaned her early. She was a person it suited. No past, only a future.

As they drew up to Belmodes, Rose said, 'I know you're a rotten little tyke in many ways, but professionally you're the tops. If I'm temporarily taken out of circulation, then you're in charge. I don't want Dagmar or Shirley.'

'But what could take you out, Rose?'

'Like being murdered or taken in by the police,' said Rose, getting out of the car.

As Gabriel trailed behind her boss's resolute stride she ought to have felt angry at the words of abuse, but she knew that they represented Rose's own fury and fear and she felt sympathy.

'At this rate, I many not be able to behave badly to her.'

AT THE entrance to Rose's office a plainclothes policewoman was standing. She spoke to Rose and the two women went into Rose's office.

Gabriel hurried up to try to hear what was said, but the door closed in her face.

After a short interval, the two came out again. As Rose left she cast a meaning glance at Gabriel, but she did not speak.

All that day Rose did not come back, nor was there any message.

Gabriel carried out Rose's instructions and kept the process of work going, ignoring the intense excitement of all the women. The sense of violence and anger, together with passionate interest, spilled out all over the place.

This is what it is like being on the outside of a murder case, thought Gabriel. Close to, yet outside, and it's not good.

'Don't you think someone should go to tell Steve that his mother is not there?' she said to Dagmar, as the day drew in.

'You do it.'

Gabriel picked up the telephone. 'Hook Road School, isn't it? I'll ask for the headmistress.'

A few years ago she might have found this impossible, the old London County Council preferring to keep its heads of schools at a distance without a telephone. This had changed; Miss Fraser could be reached.

She put her problem, then listened to the answer, her face changing. Then she put the receiver down, turning towards Dagmar.

'He isn't there. They haven't seen him all day.'

FOUR

'WHAT'S SHE LIKE, then?' said John Coffin. 'I mean, to work with.'

Having had the good fortune to fall in with Gabriel outside Cat's Coffee Shop as she was on her way home, he had seized his chance and asked her for an early supper.

Gabriel carefully buttered a roll. 'She's a good employer. I have to admit it, though in many ways she's a pain.'

She chewed her way through a good piece of the roll; she had eaten little that day.

'I wouldn't want her to go to prison.'

'Hasn't come to that.'

Gabriel leaned across the table to grip his wrist. 'You'll find out for me what's going on, won't you? You promised.'

Coffin looked thoughtful. 'I might give someone a ring.' Carefully he sorted out a few chips on his plate. 'It's not my case, you understand.'

He was to find himself repeating this often as the days went by.

'I'm going down to Mouncy Street now.' He was going to collect a few possessions and move into Mrs

Lorimer's for a bit. Impossible to live in his own house as things were. One body too many. 'I'll ring from there.'

'See what you can do. Someone's got to tell her the boy's not been at school, isn't at home,' Gabriel said, as if that was what it was all about.

'I'll have a go.' He looked at his watch. 'You stay here and eat slowly. I'll be back.'

Gabriel looked at the wall. 'Can't you phone over there?'

'Too public.' She didn't have any idea of the way you eased into queries of this sort, and to have a jukebox banging out the Rolling Stones would not provide the right background.

When he had gone, Gabriel went to the telephone herself.

'Charley?' The Beatles had taken over from the Rolling Stones, but Gabriel, used to pop boiling over all around her, did not notice.

'Speaking,' he said absently. At least he had answered the telephone. Quite hard to get through to Charley sometimes; when pressed he would simply say he was thinking. She called it Charley going incognito.

'Have you heard what's happened?'

'No, what?' He had been out working all day on a commission job for a fashionable hairdresser who was creating a branch in Los Angeles. He listened while

Gabriel told him the day's events. 'You shouldn't have interfered. Stay out of it, Gaby.'

'Rose is my employer, Charley, I want to *know*. I need to know. And then there's the boy.'

'Oh, boys that age are a law unto themselves. He's got friends somewhere, I expect.'

What he said seemed to open up vistas, disquieting views into a landscape she did not like. She did not think boys did go off on their own like that.

And across her mind, like a slug, trailed a stream of unease.

'So there's this, Charley, I'll have to forget working for Touch. Rose has fixed that. For the time being I am all Rose's property.'

And what would she do with all the pretty clothes she had created, using Rose's time and Rose's machines, and which were now stored in what Charley called his Wardrobe, a deep cupboard in his studio in Mouncy Street?

'So that's all off?'

'I'm thinking it over.' She might as well let Rose have the designs, next season they would be out of date, but a price would have to be negotiated. 'Keep my products for the time being, will you?' She could hear his dog Mop barking and whining in the background. 'What's up with Mop? He's usually so quiet.'

Gabriel went back to her table, conscious that Cat had been listening, but probably couldn't make more of it than he already knew.

He leaned across the counter. 'How's Charley, then?'

So he had been listening. 'Fine.'

'Haven't seen much of him lately.'

'He's been very busy.'

Cat gave his counter a polish with a soft duster; he liked everything he owned to shine.

Gabriel sat waiting for John Coffin to come back. He was taking his time. Why didn't she go down to his house to see for herself?

But she shied away from the idea. Somehow, it wasn't a house she wanted to go into. 'Bring me another cup of coffee,' she called to Cat.

John Coffin came in just as she took a sip. Over the years, as a young detective he had lost weight at a time when a lot of men put it on, and now looked thin and wiry, reproducing in himself, as he half knew, the family look. Generations of his forebears had lived in London, with his bearing and bone structure. Genetically speaking, they were strong stock.

He sat down across the table from Gabriel, thinking what to say. As if to aid him in his thought, Cat changed the music and let a waltz in.

'One worry off your mind,' said Coffin quietly. 'They've let Rose go home. And she knows about the boy.' He picked up her coat. 'I'll see you back.'

Gabriel obeyed him, dutifully and suddenly quiet, asking no question. That ribbon of distress had knotted itself about her, tightening around her stomach which suddenly felt overfull of coffee and food.

Pictures of Lily showing that bit of bloodied rag, of Lily's face as she launched her attack on Rose, came into her mind. She recalled Rose today in the shop, how brutal she could be in attack, but how straight. And as a background she could still see those policemen going in and out of the house on Mouncy Street the day she had seen John Coffin sitting outside. In retrospect they were predators moving in to destroy a site.

So she found herself, a young hopeful woman, with Coffin holding her hand, entering a world whose nastiness would never go away now. Once seen, this world stayed with you forever.

He did take her hand as they went towards the bus. Not for the first time she wished she had a car. Might get a Mini.

'Well, talk me through it.'

'Told you.'

'No.' Her voice was firm. 'You didn't.'

Perhaps policemen never did. He could hear his colleague Jordan's voice, unemotional on the telephone, not telling all even to him.

'She's a cool one all right. Yes, here all day.' It was the way of things, always easier to get into a police station to answer questions than to get out again.

As John Coffin had listened to Jordan's voice, he had a clear picture of the scene being summoned up so that Phil Jordan must be more of an actor than he had supposed.

'In a way, the laugh was on us.'

Rose Hilaire had sat stiffly upright, feet together, hands in her lap, refusing a cigarette—'I don't smoke—' although eventually accepting a cup of tea, during the drinking of which her hand was observed to shake.

'Yes, that was Uncle Mosse's AFS tunic. He wore it when he was doing any mucky jobs. Towards the end when he slipped out of himself a bit... Perhaps he thought he still had the right to wear it. Didn't they ever give their uniforms back? Anyway, he hadn't.'

She had examined the tunic, looking at it carefully, but not touching it. She did not have to, where clothes were concerned she knew what she was talking about.

One or two other questions, of a routine kind about the house in Mouncy Street, more to keep her talking, open her up, than anything else.

They were working up to the crucial (as it was *then*) question of how and why she had come to identify the first body as Uncle Mossycop's.

Rose Hilaire herself had nothing much to say. 'I only took a quick look, he'd been dead a long time, it wasn't nice, and yet—it looked like Uncle Mosse.'

This had been a perfectly human reaction: to look quickly at a dead relative, loved or otherwise.

But they had to dig, and wanted to, because the cool Rose with the shaking hands irritated them.

All the same, it was an unusual situation they were in and they wanted an answer, said Phil Jordan to John Coffin on the telephone.

'Of course, I was not conducting the questioning, John, but I was sitting in on it.'

All this time the bodies found, one after the other, in Mouncy Street, were being examined by the pathologists. Because of the composition of the soil underneath the Mouncy Street houses, decomposition of the bodies had been swift. This had been assisted by the existence in abundance of certain forms of animal life in the foundations: ants, cockroaches and flies had done their bit, but the mice and rats had had their flesh encounters too.

The scientists were working on one place and in one way, the police in another. Between the pathologists and police communication was intermittent, for they were parted by more than space. They were separated by the figure of Mossycop. The local police know the legend of Mosse; to the scientists he was not even a name.

'Then the telephone rang,' said Jordan, 'and that set us back on our heels. Gave Rose Hilaire the laugh all right. Not that she did laugh.' Rose Hilaire had sat there, still bolt upright, to hear what they had to say. 'It wasn't Mossycop after all.' Phil Jordan went on to tell Coffin. 'Not him but someone else wearing his uniform. A young lad, a boy; probably still an adolescent and little for his age at that. Another dead kid, and all dressed up in Mosse's old clothes. That's a problem in itself.'

There was a pause.

'We told her.' Another pause. 'Then we told her about Steve being missing. And she took it all cold—she wasn't surprised.' His voice sounded shaken. 'She was not surprised.'

John Coffin let this scene run through in his mind like a bit of film while he walked beside Gabriel.

'Don't worry about Rose,' he said. 'She knows about Steve, she knows as much as anyone can know about the deaths at the moment.'

And perhaps a little more, he thought: she was not surprised.

FIVE

ROSE WAS SITTING by her big window that overlooked the Thames when Steve came home. She had a glass of gin in her hand, but she was not drinking it, just holding it as if it might offer her the cheer and support that she might not otherwise find elsewhere. Gin had been the great popular comfort of Paradise Street in her childhood, gin and tea, so she took it as someone from another background might have made a dish of bread and milk.

She heard his key in the door, and sat alert. She knew she had made a mistake in not showing more surprise to the police. They had noticed and she had seen them notice.

Steve went quietly into the kitchen, she heard him opening the refrigerator door.

Hungry. But of course, he wouldn't have eaten.

'Steve?'

He didn't answer, naturally not. But he stopped what he was doing and came into the room. That much relationship she still had with him, she thought. His feet in the heavy studded boots he insisted on wearing, clumsy on his thin ankles, marked the pale waxed wood of her floor. Normally she would have screamed at him for the minute splinters she knew he must be creating, but now she kept her anger for other matters.

'Where have you been?'

No answer.

She looked at the huge sandwich in his hand. 'Wherever you go, they don't feed you.'

She saw him flinch; she'd scored a hit, then. It gave her no comfort. 'So what have you been doing?'

'Just walking.'

A little grudging speech was allowed, then.

'You know you put me in a bad position going off like that. I was told by the police in the station.' He did look surprised at that. 'Yes, I was down there because they were questioning me about some old clothes. Uniform.' She looked him full in the face as she spoke. And you're not surprised either, not totally, absolutely surprised. Somewhere at the back of your eyes is a show of recognition. 'You don't ask whose clothes,' she said. 'Or why I was looking at them?'

Steve put his uneaten sandwich down on the table.

'Why don't you ask?' Rose knew she should stop, she could hear herself shouting. This was not how to behave to your young son, but there was something about Steve's behaviour now that drove her on. In his own way, he knew how to pull her strings. She lowered her voice. 'There was another body under that first poor boy's. It looked like Uncle Mosse; it was wearing his old uniform. So naturally the police thought I'd identified the wrong body as Uncle.' She added briefly, 'Well, it turns out I hadn't, not in the present state of the game. But they were his clothes.'

And why hadn't I felt that shock of surprise I should have felt? I could tell you why, Steve, but I won't because I'm afraid you might know. Because Uncle Mosse left his door unlocked all the time at the end and he did not mind who came in or out, as he said. He liked company. Who's to say who drifted in, and then drifted out? Or sometimes, did not drift out? What do you know about that world, Steve?'

'I remember that uniform,' said Steve unexpectedly. 'It was fab; it had style.'

And what did he know about style? But he did; he was her child. She knew about style, so did Steve.

'I saw you put it on once.'

'Yeah. It was great.'

So he was talking, but not saying things she wanted to hear.

'And that's why I kept you apart. He was not good for you, Steve.'

I am a grown woman, I lived in Paradise Street, I know about Uncle Mosse. Oh, perhaps they aren't bad in themselves, people like that, but they let the dirt in.

Steve shrugged. Your view; I have my own, he seemed to be saying.

Irritated, Rose returned to her main worry. 'And *where* were you walking, and why? Why not school? What excuse am I going to give there?'

Awkwardly he said, 'A person has a private life. Even a young person.'

Rose drew in a sharp breath. 'You've silenced me there, kid.'

Steve picked up his sandwich and went over to the television set where he sat eating it while he watched the news. At home the new Labour Government was settling itself in. Abroad the Americans were bombing in Vietnam, Hanoi had been hit by American fighters.

Without wanting to, Rose was drawn to watch. Mother and son sat in silence watching the scenes of violence unfold.

The violence on the screen seeped out, rambled round the room like an animal, then joined them in the seats.

On the screen a taker of LSD, the Vision-of-Hell drug, was borne off on a stretcher, after having hallucinated he could fly. They all think they've got wings, thought Rose.

'If I ever thought you were mixed up in anything bad, Steve,' she said, 'I think I'd kill you.'

Then she went and stood by the window, looking out.

I am not pregnant, I have not taken a hallucinatory drug, and I have never killed anyone.

If she said it often it might be true.

She knew that, without meaning to, she had given away a lot of her life and thought, and wished she had not.

COFFIN AND GABRIEL (it was surprising how quickly he thought of them as a couple). 'Let us—' he paused '—let's meet tomorrow.' He thought about it. Tomorrow looked like being a day with a heavy workload, nor was dinner at Mrs Lorimer's entirely to be recommended. 'Let's go to a place I know. Little Italian restaurant.' Whose proprietor was currently, as they say, in prison, but whose wife, mother and seven sisters were running the place. 'La Piazza: used to be called the Padovani.'

'Oh, I know it. I was at school with the littlest Padovani.'

'Yes, you might have been.' That made her a good decade younger than he was, but she looked it. 'As an eating place it's had its ups and downs, but it's up at the moment.' It was, in fact, better when its handsome but feckless proprietor was absent. His amours seemed to upset the cooking.

'I'll look forward to it.'

They turned the corner into the street where Gabriel lived; she had a tiny flat.

'What's she like, your boss? Really like?'

Gabriel said, 'I haven't much idea. She covers up, pretty well. Deep.'

'I've never met her,' said Coffin thoughtfully. 'I don't think.'

'Oh, you'd know if you had. You don't overlook Rose if she's around. Tall, bright blue eyes, mass of hair.'

'What colour?'

'Oh, varies—sometimes pale blonde, sometimes more honey-coloured. I've even known her red, and that only in the eighteen months I've worked for her. But she's got style. She can't make it, but she can copy it.' Gabriel spoke with feeling; she knew what she had contributed to Belmodes since she had started to work there.

'And what's she been like these last months?' What he meant was: Did she act like a woman who might know too much about a murdered boy?

'Again, hard to say.' Gabriel had been full of her own plans lately, perhaps not too observant. 'But she has seemed under pressure. Her relationship with the boy has gone to pot lately. I think we all knew that and she didn't mind showing it. Don't know what was behind it. Maybe he didn't like her friends. Or she didn't like his.'

'Think so?'

Gabriel shrugged. 'It's a funny old world—and people like Rose, well, they get mixed up in it.'

'And you? Do you get mixed up?' He didn't know where he placed Gabriel. She looked a bright, emancipated little bird, enjoying her freedom, but he thought he detected a native caution underneath her swinging exterior.

'In and out,' said Gabriel.

'I won't ask questions.'

'You already are,' said Gabriel drily.

'You'll still have dinner with me?'

'As long as you don't ask me who I voted for in the General Election.' (The country was still sorting itself out after the Election.)

'Who *did* you vote for?'

'Oh, I didn't bother.'

Coffin was shocked. Far away and long ago seemed the world after the War, into which he had emerged out of the army with the feeling that his vote and the new Labour Government would rebuild England. He still voted Labour, but he was no longer sure why. But not to use a vote, that was what had changed.

A gap opened between them, and they both knew it was called age.

But physical attraction could jump that gap like an electric spark and did so effortlessly. He put his arm round her and they walked on.

'How did you feel about me being a policeman?'

A bus passed them, bringing with it a flurry of dry dust from the gutter.

'I never forget it for a minute,' said Gabriel. 'Any more questions?' I'm a slum kid, her eyes were saying, you know that, do you think we forget policemen? What's democracy in Paradise Street? Not policemen. This was not a question, it was an answer. Nevertheless, she would go on knowing him.

They parted with barely a word, but with a strength of unexpressed feeling. They would meet, they would go on meeting, but already they were on opposite sides.

Rose had enrolled Gabriel, with a jump of surprise the girl admitted it. While she had not been looking where she was going, Rose had quietly taken her support. Rose and Belmodes, it was then.

It was as if she had smelt a meal cooking in the next room; it might not be a meal she wanted to eat, but already it was nourishing her.

John Coffin did not know he was on the wrong side yet, not having so far met Rose Hilaire, but he too realized that there might be a fight ahead.

'See you tomorrow.'

'As ever is.' Gabriel disappeared into her own flat, which was minute, one room and a bathroom, but which she shared with no one. The first upward step of any born in Paradise Street was a room of one's own. Very few people had seen inside Gabriel's flat, because that was the other rule for escapers from Paradise Street: do not let the world outside get past your front door. 'Don't expect too much of me. Got a busy day tomorrow.'

IT WAS ALWAYS busy at this time of the year in Belmodes, preparing the collection for the next season. Murder or not, it had to go on, and next day it did, Rose saw to that, although she was not herself.

Rose Hilaire had a waking dream, one which followed her into sleep and came out again on the other side to stay with her all day, going with her into Belmodes side by side like a fellow worker.

As she slept in her Italian-designed tube steel bed with the iron-grey duvet, she felt sure that Steve in the room across the corridor must know who was there with her, and as she went to work next day, she felt sure that everyone must see what she was dragging with her. Her nightmare self, her horrible double.

In this dream she was outside herself, yet watching a person who must be herself strangling an adolescent boy.

What she saw was detailed and specific, nothing vague or fancy. Just a pair of hands, reaching out at the end of her arms from her shoulders to grip a neck. Not exactly the sort of thought you wanted to pass on to the police at a time when two boys' bodies had been found. Yet one that was hard to keep to yourself, she could feel it bursting out all over her. Like a virulent disease. Someone was bound to notice. Excuse me, they might say, you have death all over your face, it could be serious.

At work next day, discussing time-sheets and piece-work rates with Dagmar, she could feel her skin irritating her.

She put her hand up to her face.

'What is the matter with you, Rose? You keep touching your face.' Dagmar was irritable.

'I'm having a little trouble with it.'

Dagmar did not answer. She had known Rose since before Rose was born, and had long since resolved to think nothing about Rose except what suited her. It did not suit her now to observe the emotional turmoil inside Rose. Herself the illegitimate daughter of a Danish sailor who had spent one month in Paradise Street before taking ship for ever, she had built herself a firmly structured life which could withstand all but atomic bombardment.

'You've got your warpaint on,' she said.

Rose was wearing a tulip-red trouser suit, diamond earrings and a large aquamarine ring.

She grunted. 'If I didn't believe clothes helped, then I wouldn't be in this business.' She sighed. 'But who said work helps?' and pushed away from her desk. 'Are the police still in the washroom?'

Dagmar's expression did not change from her usual workday look of reserve. 'The police have gone, but the washroom's locked up and no one can get in. The girls are having to use the public lavatory on the corner and they don't like it.'

'They won't go on strike, will they?' Rose feared strikes even more than bankruptcy or the plague.

'I haven't heard them mention it,' said Dagmar in a level voice.

Rose got up and walked to the window. Her suit made of nylon had stuck to her and outlined her figure. Out of the window, she could see the street outside, with one of her own vans drawing away from the kerb. A smaller delivery van from a wholesaler was just moving into her unloading yard. That would be the Italian silk jersey arriving. Good news on an ordinary day, a delight to the eye. This was not an ordinary day.

'We don't know a lot, do we?' she said, fixing her eyes on a policeman in uniform who was walking by.

They were in the middle of the case, working in a building where bloodstained clothing had been found, and where two people whom the police had questioned about a missing boy had more than passing contact, yet they knew less than anyone.

'Any news about Ephraim?'

'Not that I know. Anyway, Lily isn't in today.'

'Just as well,' said Rose uneasily. 'It's a difficult situation there. See she's paid, though, won't you?'

'You're a good employer,' said Dagmar grudgingly.

'Better than Grandpa? He kept a sweatshop if anyone did. Changed days, couldn't behave like that now. But I'm standing on his shoulders, Dagmar.'

'And wouldn't he have loved it.' For Dagmar that was a show of humour. Since her mother had been a jolly lady, her missing father must have been a dour Dane indeed if inheritance had anything to do with it.

Rose came back into the room, and sat down at her desk. 'You don't think there's any special reason for Lily being away?'

'Such as?'

'Like Ephraim being found?'

'Did cross my mind.'

'You know something,' said Rose suddenly.

'Not know. Saw.'

'Oh, come on.'

'You didn't drive down Mouncy Street from the main road this morning?'

'No. Came round the other way from Decimus Street.' She did not say that she was avoiding passing the house in Mouncy Street, but they both knew she was, and had been every day.

'Two police cars; and an ambulance. Drove off as I went past.' Dagmar cycled from her flat in one of the new highrise blocks.

'Same house as before?' asked Rose carefully. The one I used to own, she meant, the one the copper bought.

'That or the next one. Both been empty.'

'Well, thanks for telling me.' For Dagmar it had been tactfully done. 'We'll wait and see.' And it might mean nothing. But the cameo of death formed in front of her eyes, small, brightly lit and detailed. She closed her eyes.

'I'll get you a cup of tea,' said Dagmar.

'No. I've got to see Gaby. She's probably outside now.'

'She can wait. You'd better tell me what's upsetting you.'

In a low tone, Rose said, 'Do you believe in anyone fantasizing murder? Have you ever heard of anyone doing that?'

Gaby who was outside, heard the word murder and stayed to listen. It was wrong to do it, she knew, but she could not stop herself. She could not hear anything, of course, as Rose's voice dropped and was interrupted by the rumble of Dagmar's, but she heard enough.

The question was whether she should tell anyone or no one what she had heard.

That question was decided for her in a most terrible way.

WHEN THE rumour reached Gabriel she began to realize what she would say to John Coffin.

Rose had said, in a terrified whisper: 'Can you fantasize a murder? Feel sure that you saw one happen?'

She didn't hear Dagmar's response. But Rose said: 'I think I might be the killer. I was inside it, and outside it, at the same time.'

What Dagmar said then sounded like 'a dream'; she couldn't hear what answer Rose made to that, but she heard the words 'missing' and 'blood'.

Gabriel tried to slot this into what the new death was all about; she was deeply troubled. She slipped out for a cup of coffee with Charley in his studio next to Belmodes; it was one of his days to be there. She had been able to tell that by the sight of his motorbike outside. He flitted about on this machine (which obsessed him) wearing a helmet and goggles so that Gabriel called him The Invisible Man. On wheels.

'What do you think I should do?' she said to Charley. 'You always give me good advice: give me some now.'

'Do I?'

'I think so.'

A minute ticked by while Charley said nothing.

Gabriel went on, 'And then I saw her that night, remember? In Mouncy Street. I told you. She was behaving oddly.'

'Which night was that? Remind me.'

'The night I worked late on my own. That was why I had a taxi. You had a job in Paris.'

'Brussels,' said Charley absently. 'I told you Brussels.'

Gabriel irritated him by the way she could get something nearly right but not quite.

Charley sat silent, then took a deep breath. 'Tell them. You asked me, I say: Tell.'

By lunch-time the rumour was a hard story. So Gabriel knew she had to tell. And to her, in her present mood, that meant tell Coffin.

SIX

'SINCE YOU ASK about the boy,' said Phil Jordan to his friend John Coffin, 'I will tell you.'

'But I didn't,' Coffin said. They were drinking in the Red Anchor; it was noon or just past, and still a full working day.

'Oh, come on, that's why you asked me for a drink. And I'll have another. You owe me.'

'Oh, all right.' John Coffin got up.

'Well, you've got a right to know. He's in your garden. Three feet down and under a rose-bush. Identified by his clothes. But someone from the family will have to have a look.'

Coffin swallowed his drink. It went down badly, sour to his taste. His throat tightened.

'When?'

Jordan shrugged. 'Probably soon after he went missing. The forensics will take time.' And hedge their bets, then.

'And how long is that?'

'Almost three weeks.' He added, 'Just after the Bank Holiday. Labour Day.' He had got the impression that for some reason this was important, but he did not know why.

They drank in silence for a minute or two.

Coffin said, 'I had the house then. Hadn't moved in, but I got the keys before the holiday. *My* house.'

'I know.'

'I had a look at the garden. He must have been there then.'

'Looks like it.'

'And the Big S?'

'Sexual attack? Forensics say no obvious sign of it. But in my book it has to be there, one way or another. Yes, there was certainly a sexual gratification for the killer, whether man, woman or child.'

'You mean that? Every word, every child?'

Jordan shrugged. 'They're at it younger and younger. We've both had cases.'

'Damn.'

Jordan said, 'To tell you the truth, I don't think we're making too good a job of it.'

Coffin looked at him. Not like Jordan to be self-critical.

'It slips away from us. As soon as we think we're making progress we seem to lose our grip. The forensics, the laboratory stuff—all the stuff we've taken in—soil, clothing fragments, even some flakes found on the first boy—they look promising, but we don't get any further. They don't point anywhere we can find. Or not without a bit of help. Perhaps this new body will give something extra.' He frowned. Poor little beast. Perhaps his body would speak for him. It might have a lot to say. 'I hear they've got a problem to worry at there, but details I don't know.'

'It's lousy business, so it is.'

Jordan sighed and took a drink. 'Old Mossycop's the problem, he let anyone in to that place. Anyone could have had access. Got hold of key, kept it. He didn't seem to care. When someone like Mosse, who's had a kind of public face, goes wrong, he really beats all.'

'Think so?' It didn't seem entirely the problem to Coffin.

Jordan thought again. 'No, it's not just that. I think the old man isn't handling it well. Can't seem to take the emotion. Remember when Tom Banbury went off it all? Lost his grip?'

'He came back,' said Coffin quickly, defensively. 'One or two good results after that.'

'What's happened to him?'

'Retired early. He died a year ago,' said Coffin shortly; he had liked his first boss.

'Do you still keep in with the great man Dander?'

'Yes.' Commander Dander had been, still was, Coffin's patron. You needed a patron. Jordan knew all that, he was just asking for asking's sake.

'You're well in there. Gone right to the top, the lucky bastard.'

'He's got a bit grand for me.'

'Not what I hear.'

They drank for a moment before Jordan returned to what really worried him about his boss's handling of the case.

'The trouble is he can't talk to people. Not properly. Question, yes. Talk, no.'

'Tom Banbury couldn't.' Couldn't or wouldn't. 'In the end, I think, it killed him.' Cancer of the larynx cannot come by accident. Or is it falling into the old sin of hubris to say you can will your own death?

The real trouble with old Tom had been that when he came into contact with the evil mind, the scheming, devious, manipulative mind of some murderers, he could not bear it.

'Someone ought to talk to the family connections,' Coffin said aloud. 'People like Lily Bates.'

SOMEONE OUGHT to talk to Lily Bates, yes, that was what he had said and meant, but it might not have been him if he hadn't seen her for himself that afternoon between five and six, the period between Hook Road School closing and Rose leaving her office at Belmodes; the time Steve would have made his own.

She was standing face to face with a boy in the public park at the end of Decimus Street. He recognized her at once because Gabriel had pointed her out to him and he thought the boy must be young Hilaire. It was a conjunction of two people at once unlikely and yet inevitable. Of course, she'd get at the boy if she could.

He stopped to watch. Where they were talking was a children's playground, not much used; a small desolation of climbing frames and broken swings. The barbarians had passed over it and moved on.

Afterwards he had to explain why he was there, and found it hard. I was just there, he said, but it wasn't true. He had gone there on purpose. Not thinking he could see them, but thinking he would see something. Driven there by some distant memory from his youth.

It was a place where boys and vagrants went, had been for years. One of several in the district but the one nearest to Mouncy Street. This was probably in his mind.

Lily and the boy were standing by an old iron playhorse which had once been painted dark green but now was blotched with rust.

Blessed with excellent long-range vision, he stood outside the play area, observing them. The boy had his back to him but he could see Lily's face and she was doing the talking.

He stood there watching. 'Wish I could lip-read.'

But just watching was telling him something. They moved as in a dance.

Now the boy Steve was doing the talking while Lily was listening, and that surprised him. The boy was going on at length with apparent fluency. From Lily's back he could tell nothing.

A shame not to be able to hear, but he knew if he took one more step towards them the scene would break up and he would lose them.

In the end it was the woman who gave ground and the boy who stayed.

No doubt he should report it, and probably he would.

But, after all, what could he say? That he had seen the two talking?

And it wasn't his case.

NOT HIS CASE, but his feet thought otherwise. They followed Lily; sometimes, as detective, your feet do know best. He had to hope so, because his feet appeared to be following Lily, carrying him with them, willy-nilly.

He went after Lily, not sure exactly what he would do. He followed her down one quiet suburban street after another till they approached the busy main road. Then she stopped and turned around.

'You're following me. You ought to be ashamed of yourself. Go away or I'll call the police.' Her eyes flicked towards the main road where a uniformed constable stood. She had led him there neatly.

'I'm sorry if I frightened you.'

She thought about him. 'You're a policeman yourself.'

'I thought you'd recognize it.' The policeman at the corner was looking interested.

'Don't count on that, son. Or being liked the more because of it.'

'I don't.'

The uniformed policeman had begun a slow, thoughtful walk in their direction. Explanations could be made, but might not be easy. Not his case.

'So what do you want?' Gabriel would have recognized that Lily was in one of her aggressive moods; they alternated with gentle or more co-operative states. 'I suppose I ought to expect to be bullied. Spied on.'

'No one's doing that.' Not strictly true, he thought; no wonder some people have mixed feelings about us. I did exactly what she said. Still, my motives were good. He added politely, 'Mrs Bates?'

'I'm in mourning, did you know that? My little nephew has been found. Dead. Murdered. More like a grandson than a nephew he was to me.'

'I'm sorry.'

By now she'd had a good look at him. 'I've known you. I've seen you with Gaby.'

'That's right.'

'Does she know about Ephraim?'

'Not yet.' But she'd have to be told.

'I thought she didn't. Or she'd have let me know. In a kinder way than you lot did.'

'It had to be the police tell,' he said deprecatingly. 'Where do you live, Mrs Bates?'

She nodded to one of the row of tidy brick houses.

'Can we go in the house and talk? That's all I wanted.'

Also this young police constable was getting closer. Lily too had noticed the policeman by now and perhaps did not want to encounter him. 'Yes,' she said quickly, and led the way to the house without hesitation.

Inside, Lily's house was sunlit and quiet. She led him straight into an old-fashioned kitchen where a coal range gave out a dull red glow. He could smell cooking.

'Always keep a casserole going in the oven ready for when I come home from work. Always been a working woman. Had to be, and keep my family comfortable.'

'You a widow?'

'No, I've still got Dad, but he doesn't count for much now, poor love, he's gone a little bit silly.'

'Ah.'

'He can't walk, though, his legs have gone, so you needn't start having suspicious thoughts about him. He's upstairs now, asleep. Or thinking. He does lot of thinking even if he can't say what. As harmless as a baby. More harmless than some babies I've known.'

'I don't know much about babies,' said Coffin humbly.

'Oh, it's the ones that have a sharp look to them that you've got to watch out for. They're the bad ones. Look like little old men, they do, sometimes. Then you've got to watch what they grow up like.'

'Poor little things.' He felt a serious sympathy for the little ones looking like their own grandfathers; he had probably been such a one himself. 'And what about your nephew, Ephraim? Was he one of the sharp ones?'

Lily didn't answer; she was bent down getting the casserole from the oven. The fragrant steam made his mouth water.

After a bit she said. 'I don't know about Ephraim. I loved him, so it was harder to see.'

'He lived with you?'

'No. With his mother and stepfather and his grandmother. Nice old soul, but you have to think for her.'

Lily looked as though she had been thinking for her whole family all her life; she was younger, by far, than she appeared.

'Didn't he have anyone closer?'

'Not that were any good to him. He was born out of wedlock.' She used the old phrase. 'His real father's in the Merchant Navy, and when we'll see him next, I couldn't say. Off the coast of West Africa when I last heard from him, and that wasn't so very recent. As for his mother...' She shrugged. 'Here today and gone tomorrow, that one. Moved in with a boy that's got a group. Then they got married. So there's a kind of stepfather.'

She made it sound like a disease. She had the casserole lid off and was stirring its contents. 'Lot of them around at the moment.'

He took the spoon out of her hand and laid it on the table. 'And what about Steve Hilaire? Is he a sharp one growing up bad?'

Lily put the lid on the casserole, and the casserole in the oven. She shrugged.

'You spoke to him.' Coffin reminded her.

'Have *you* spoken to him?' Coffin shook his head. 'Perhaps you should. Try it for yourself, see where it gets you. Have a try. I had to speak to him, to find out what he knew about Ephraim; after all, he had Ephraim's boots.'

'And?'

'He makes me angry.'

'How is that?'

'He won't answer questions. None of my Why questions. Nor How. Just didn't answer. Or couldn't.'

'He seemed to be talking.'

Lily gave him a look telling of her own sharpness. 'Oh, you saw that, did you? Pity you can't lip-read.'

Coffin had often thought the same himself. 'He was talking. But there's talking and saying. He wasn't saying. He talked about nothing.'

'Absolutely nothing?'

'He talked about himself. That was nothing to me. I wanted to know when he'd last seen Ephraim. Where he'd last seen him. What they'd done together. The places they went to. Were they true friends? And why?' She shook her head. 'Nothing. He didn't know. Or couldn't remember. But about himself he practically told me what he had for breakfast. I'd like to be a policeman, he said. Or if not a policeman, then a doctor.'

'I wonder why.'

'So he could make trouble for people,' said Lily sourly.

'Is that really you talking, Lily Bates? Saying these things?'

There were angry tears in Lily's eyes. 'I used to like the little beggar. Time was when he was always around my house with Ephraim. I thought they were pals, real pals. I knew he kept it from his mother. I suppose I ought to have realized that if a boy could do that, then he wouldn't be open to anyone else. I wish I hadn't spoken to him now.'

'You'd have done better to leave him alone.'

'I wanted to know for myself, hard and clear, with my own ears what he knew about Ephraim.'

Coffin said, 'I think you took a risk, talking to him in the park.'

He did not amplify nor did Lily ask the nature of that risk, but it was a comment he profoundly believed, an emotion rather than a rational thought. He was working on it. But what he seemed to be sensing was that the boy was dangerous.

Somehow or the other, he was not sure how, she had dished him out a plate of stew and he was sitting eating it.

The kitchen was a homely, comfortable room. Everything that could be polished was polished, but nothing was new, all the furniture and equipment settled into their accustomed places as of long habit. It was cosy.

I'm setting Lily in her context, Coffin thought. And Ephraim too. These are ordinary people. Steve and Rose are not ordinary people.

'What did they do together? Any idea at all?' He was trying to get a picture of the life that Steve and Ephraim had had together. From that life seemed to have come death.

'Oh, they were always out. Away and off together. But I didn't know where. You know lads. But they often came back here for their tea.' Rose, her tone implied, was a poor cook and a worse mother.

'And they'd talk? So you knew what they got up to?'

'Not lately. Not the last year. Shut down, they both did.'

'And that worried you?'

'Yes. It did. But just lately—' she hesitated '—just lately, I've wondered if Steve *ever* gave much away.' Once again she hesitated. 'He's a manager. He can pull strings.'

'Manipulative, you mean?'

The word was alien to her and she looked doubtful. 'If you say so.'

'Thanks for telling me all this; it's what I wanted to know.'

'You're a nice young man. I wouldn't talk to everyone like I've talked to you.'

'I know that, Mrs Bates.'

'He saw too much of old Mosse. That house, it was a disgrace. Attracted the dregs.'

'Yes. And I wanted to know about that too.'

'A disgrace. He let himself and the house go. I hope you'll be happy in it.'

'I shall try to be,' said Coffin soberly. If he got the chance.

Lily saw him to the front door.

'They were only kids,' she said despairingly.

'Only kids,' said Coffin. 'Steve still is.' But a kid with Uncle Mosse and his house in his background, a house in which murder had been done.

Uncle Mosse, retired eccentric, and a house in Mouncy Street; genetics and environment, the two strands in making a person.

And you had to take Rose Hilaire into the equation.

She came into it, mercilessly when he had heard what Gabriel had to say.

SEVEN

IT WAS a warm evening. Suddenly and unseasonably warm. Coffin found it hard to tuck into Mrs Lorimer's cold beef and salad after having eaten Lily Bates's stew. Nor did he fancy it greatly; after some years away from Mrs Lorimer's hotel and of looking after himself, eating exactly what he liked, it was hard to get used to her iron hand with a potato.

All over Greenwich and down into Deptford and along in Woolwich, people were protesting at the sudden heat. It was unnatural, they said, hot days ought to start gradually, beginning with dawn, but this one had hit them suddenly between four and five in the afternoon. By six-thirty it was hot, with the temperature still rising. For some unexplained reason many housewives had cooked beef in one form or another that night and Coffin was probably lucky to find his second supper was cold, for all over South London people were pushing back plates.

'And what are you doing this evening?' asked Mrs Lorimer. She was virtually retired these days, her hotel (where Coffin had once lived) turned into small flats over whose tenants she kept a stern eye. A favourite few like John Coffin could still be housed *en*

pension, as it were. It was because of the overpower-
ing force of this favouritism that he had chosen to
move elsewhere, making the demands of his job the
pretext.

'I'm going to my evening class.'

'Oh, which one? German, or the other one?'

'The family history one.' He could have lied, but he
usually found himself speaking the truth to Mrs Lorimer; it was another reason for moving out.

'*Still* intent on finding your lost brother?' She shook
her head. 'A waste of time.'

'I don't think so. And I enjoy it.' He did. If he
hadn't been a detective he might have been a histo-
rian. Indeed, there was a sense in which he was a his-
torian: he loved investigating source material, going
back to the originals, and patiently fitting one piece of
evidence into the pattern with another.

'It's the girl that teaches the class: the one with red
hair.'

'No, it isn't.' Another thing she disapproved of was
his passionate interest in the other sex. But he did like
the young woman, a hoyden from Somerville who
gambled on the horses and was always broke.

'All right, what are you doing this week?' It was a
challenge; not for nothing had Mrs Lorimer been a
formidable ARP warden in the war, and later a JP.

'Parish registers. And I've done my homework.'

She leaned forward. 'Mark my words, no good will come of it.' Then she relented: 'Have some apple tart?'

'No, thank you.' Her iron hand was even harder on the pastry, and affected its colour as well so that it looked dark and oppressed. 'Too hot.'

'I know what's the matter with you: those dead boys.'

'Not my case,' he muttered.

'No. But your house. And you can't stop thinking about it.' Well, that was true enough. 'And you mind, reminds you of that other case.'

At the beginning of his career, a friend of young John Coffin's had been a multiple murderer, and he had learnt something of their nature. They were a strange breed, these killers who might or might not know their victims, but for whom the victim filled a need. Between victim and murderer there was a match, too; they slotted into position in each other's lives like template and pattern.

Other things he knew as well, and meant to look out for. Like the shadow such killers cast on others.

'Do you ever hear from Stella Pinero?'

He had fallen in love too at that time. He shook his head. 'No.' That was in character: Stella did not look back.

'She's certainly done well,' said Mrs Lorimer grudgingly.

'She's a good actress.' Perhaps even a great one; he always went to see her perform. Thus aiding his education because Stella was stretching her powers in the classics: Hedda Gabler, Lady Macbeth, St Joan.

'You know Angel House is being turned into a Museum of the Theatre?'

He nodded silently. Of course he knew. Rachel Esthart, a famous actress of her day, and a patron of Stella Pinero's just as the then Chief Inspector Dander had been of the young Coffin, had left her Greenwich house to Stella.

'Now there *was* an actress. Better than Stella, to my mind.'

'Different.'

'More heart. Shame she died so soon after that come-back.' Mrs Lorimer was a keen student of the theatre and could swap phrases like 'come-back' and 'a turkey' and 'papering the house' with the best. 'Seemed as if she had that one last flare of light before she went out.'

Mrs Lorimer chewed her way through her own helping of apple tart.

'Oh, that reminds me. That other young woman rang up.'

'What other one?'

'The new one: Gabriel.'

'Yes, not my new one.' But he knew she would be if he could work it. 'What did she want?'

'She wants to talk to you.' Mrs Lorimer's eyebrows rose. 'We thought of better excuses in my day. You're to telephone her.'

THEY MET, by arrangement, outside the entrance to the school where his evening class was held. With the inevitability of certain aspects of life, this was, of course, Hook Road School.

'Coming in?' he said. A few drops of rain were falling from the overheated sky.

'I don't think so,' Gabriel responded nervously. 'I went to this school myself.'

'So did I.' Another thing they had in common. Hook Road graduates, both.

'Let's walk up and down while I tell you.'

She was nervous as she handed out the story, but she told it vividly, her body unconsciously acting out the story so that he could almost see and hear Rose and Dagmar.

'Charley said I must tell you.'

'Calm down, Gabriel.' He put his arm round her thin shoulder. 'Nice scent you're wearing.'

'It's a new one.' She relaxed a little. 'American. They're making good scents now. Quite different from a French scent, isn't it?... So what do you think?' Her voice rose. 'I think she's killed someone. Perhaps Ephraim. Or anyway, seen a killing.'

'Seen a killing,' repeated Coffin. 'Well, she could have done. Thought of asking?'

'*No!*'

In the end, someone will, he thought. 'Why have you told me?'

'You're a policeman.'

'Not my case.' That was going to be written on his heart.

'Still—I saw her in Mouncy Street one night,' said Gabriel suddenly. 'I thought she was drunk. She was near your house, she sat on the wall.'

'When was this?'

'I can't be sure. But it could have been about the time Ephraim disappeared.'

'Who else have you told?'

'Just Charley.'

His grip on her arm tightened. 'Gaby, let me explain something: this is a major case. A multiple murder case.' A few heavy spots of rain were falling on the pavements like coins. 'A lot of people will be involved. There is an Investigating Officer—he's a kind of control figure; he has an Incident Room. But there is also a scene-of-the-crime officer, a photographer, a pathologist. Various forensic people, and probably a search team. That's a lot of people, Gaby, and I am not one of them.'

'Still...' she said again.

'I am busy on my own work: I am part of a team, legging it around London, working undercover.' Gently he said. 'So I've got other things on my mind, Gaby.'

Triumphantly she said, 'But I know.' She corrected herself. 'We know that you've seen Lily. And you were seen talking to your pal Jordan who is on the case. We watch you, you know.' She nodded. 'You are interested. We know.'

Coffin stared at her; her little face was excited and interested. Intent, was another word.

It was at this moment, with a faint feeling that made the hair on his head prickle, that Coffin got the first intimation that even if it was not his case, he himself was in it.

Right in it.

We know, she'd said. Damn you, Gabriel, you've opened my eyes and no one enjoys that.

He was seeing it all so differently from Gabriel; he was seeing it from the other side of the mirror.

And he was looking at his own face.

Of course Jordan was taking time off to talk to him, and of course he was observed, probably on all sides.

It was his house.

That investigating team he'd talked about, they were probably passionately interested in him.

In the nicest possible way, of course. Young Coffin? Decent chap, this business can't be anything to do with him. Still, we'd better look.

You bet.

He wiped his forehead.

Hot. Was it getting hotter?

As THE heat of the evening mounted, Rose Hilaire opened all the windows in her sitting-room to let air in.

There was a lot of bad feeling floating around her house and by opening the windows she hoped to let it out. The smell that floated back from the river with its docks and factories was unpleasant, like her life at present.

One chink of light had appeared, however: Steve was talking to her. Not a lot, not saying much, but offering observations voluntarily, as if there was a relationship between them.

Not necessarily that of mother and son; Steve had detached himself from that hook and would never be hung on it again.

Just as well, perhaps, but for Rose, not so easy. One tiny little fragment of her would always be a mother.

But at least there was a kind of to and fro between them, more like a tennis match perhaps than a genuine conversation, with words being patted back and forth, but Rose at least was grateful for it.

She leaned out of the window, trying to enjoy the fresher air; a scent of burning rubber drifted in. To the west was a soap factory; she could smell that too. 'Good old Deller's,' she murmured.

Steve was sitting in front of the television set watching a pop show.

'What's that you're listening to?'

'"Ready, Steady. Go."' Pretty Things.'

'Noisy.'

'I like them. Better than the Stones.'

'I thought it was all the Beatles.'

'Oh—' he was dismissive '—wouldn't miss them.'

'Time for you to go to bed.'

He got up almost at once without argument. In that kind of way he was never any trouble. It was good behaviour. Or, looked at from another point of view, it was most abnormal.

'Good night,' she said to his back. From the back he looked just like anyone else.

What she longed to ask him was: 'Have I ever been missing for any time, Steve? Been away and not come back when I should? Acted strange? Have I ever come back with blood on me?

But these were questions you did not ask.

Because he might say: 'Yes, Mum, once or twice you did. And I happen to know it was you that put Ephraim's boots in my bag.'

She sat back in her chair by the window and let the hot air play over her face.

She relaxed and her mind ran free.

Soon she felt a different person. Or the same person in another skin.

THE MURDERER came out and sniffed the air temporarily. Hot. There was something stimulating about the warmed air so heavy with the smells of living. For the murderer it summoned up memories of shared moments. These were valuable, photographs in an album. A black album.

One or two anxieties came with the memories.

A pity about the boy's boots. That was a mistake. Looked a good idea. Wasn't. The murderer thought about it, still finding it almost as amusing as it had seemed at the time; the murderer's sense of humour was childlike, adolescent at the best, but secretive. All the best jokes were private.

A joke against authority that now didn't look so good. The trouble with being what you were was that although your judgement was impeccable, the rest of the world just didn't always know it. They would *never* know the utter thrill. It had been spicy, really rich, having the body 'at home', as it were, over the holiday, when Belmodes was empty. The body at rest in the cupboard in the women's room. Then, before the holiday ended, removed, which involved a certain amount of dragging. It would be better to be stronger in the arms, help could be summoned, but some tasks one did on one's own. Leaving the pants in the cupboard was possibly a nothing, and picking up the reel of red thread in the boots simply accident, done goodness knows how. The world, of course, would look for plan and purpose here, not knowing how much a creature of serendipity you were, not knowing, just doing.

They'd learn. You were what you were, and the world would just have to learn.

Rose woke up from her sleep (if it had been a true sleep) and stirred. She thought she could hear someone moving about. Or was it just noises in the skull? She had plenty of those too.

'Is that you, Steve?'

Silence.

EIGHT

IT WAS not too hot to sleep: in Coffin's life it had never been too hot or too cold or too anything to find oblivion. Sleep always came to him easily and quickly, very often unexpectedly, burying him when he wasn't looking. Death would be like that for him, he always supposed. But tonight his thoughts were stamping around his mind wearing heavy boots.

They were beating a clear path. The path towards Uncle Mosse of Mouncy Street. Turn which way you would, Edward Mosse, retired and dotty, and his house in Mouncy Street were always there, a kind of terrible citadel.

He knew without doubt it was a path he was going to walk: the path to old Mossycop.

The place was vital.

Victims sought out their killers. Yes, that was acknowledged. You had to look for a pairing between murderer and victim.

But places, too, sometimes cried out for their crime.

The house on Mouncy Street had been such a place. He could see that now.

Created by Ted Mosse, a lover of uniforms, not too honest, deceased.

It was, after all, no real mistake that his body had been falsely identified as being there. Uncle Mosse had *wanted* to be dead there, and since he couldn't achieve it for himself, his clothes had done it for him.

There are no accidents in murder. It all comes about as deliberately, if unconsciously, contrived.

Then Coffin thought: No that's a bit fancy, boy. But he did have fancy thoughts sometimes, nor were they always wrong.

A fancy thing popped into his mind then, handed to him by the tutor of his evening class.

When you don't know where to begin your investigation about your family, she had said, start talking to the last generation back, then the one before if there are any survivors. They were there, raid their memories, make your start with them.

Get in touch with the eldest living contacts, Marina Marsden had said, her big blue eyes sparkling with enthusiasm. No wonder the class loved her.

He started with himself.

I am the first living contact to consult, Coffin thought, lying back in his hard bed under Mrs Lorimer's roof.

He began to assemble what he remembered about the house in Mouncy Street as he had first known it.

Old Mosse saved three people from a burning house in the Blitz but was a thieving rat otherwise. Was he a grand old man or a proper perisher?

Then, just for a moment, unpredictably, his unknown sibling was in the room with him. He had taken
to doing this lately. His appearance varied. Sometimes he looked like John Coffin himself, sometimes
he was more like what Coffin remembered of his
mother, but he was always young. He was ageless. Sir
James Barrie would have known him for a Lost Boy.

He did not always have a voice, but he always had
a point of view. 'You hardly knew old Mosse, remember,' he now pointed out. 'He hardly left the
house by the time you got round to him.'

They don't wear knickers in Paradise Street, they
had said in Mouncy Street. But life had caught up with
them. No one wore knickers any more. They wore
tights, and what they wore underneath that no one had
told Coffin.

'I'm going down Mouncy Street,' he said to his sibling. 'And down Decimus Street and then to Paradise
Street. I'm going to ask all the old 'uns.'

If there were any left. But there were. When he had
one of these fancy feelings he was never entirely
wrong.

He had always liked Decimus Street, it was a decent little street without the glamour of being wicked
like Paradise Street.

Mouncy Street and Decimus Street and Paradise
Street formed three sides of a square with all the
backyards running together. The fourth side of the

square was occupied by a gas-works whose gasometer looked down on its neighbours. During the war it had been a dangerous neighbour, but no bomb had fallen on it, although fire-bombs had spattered all over Mouncy Street and Decimus Street. The inhabitants were used to the smell, which mixed in nicely with the odours from Deller's soap factory and the mingled scents from the river. It was a homely smell, they hardly noticed it.

The smell was as familiar to Coffin as anyone else. One of those things you forget about when away, then meet with surprised pleasure on a return. Now he fancied himself a connoisseur of the smell, able to distinguish between its elements. Mouncy Street had more of the river in its atmosphere, Decimus Street more of the gasometer, while Paradise Street, as was to be expected, was altogether richer and racier on account of the cats'-meat man who boiled up his ware in an old stable in the road. He had survived two world wars and a slump. There was never any shortage of cats in the neighbourhood; they too added their smell to the back gardens.

No one took any notice of him when he arrived back in Mouncy Street. He was not yet known as a neighbour. His own house, at which he looked wistfully, was still in the control of his colleagues. Was it his fancy that he saw Phil Jordan staring at him morosely through an upper window? He knew he must still be an object of some interest. But his time was his own; he was off duty.

He knew that the investigation into the deaths of the young boys was proceeding slowly but methodically, building up a picture.

All the boys had died by strangling. Not manual strangulation: a lead had been drawn sharply round the neck in each case.

No. 30 Mouncy Street was his first stop because he knew already from his own observation that here lived a truly old inhabitant; Mary Adelaide Flock, who had been born twenty years before Queen Victoria died and did not count herself old yet. 'A proper old duck', she was known as locally, but she was a duck who had somehow acquired a set of sharp teeth with a bite.

Coffin had wondered how to introduce himself, but there was no need. She leaned out of her front bay-window and gave him a shout. 'Let yourself in; the door's on the latch.'

She was a large woman, wearing a blue cotton dress with two woollen cardigans, one white, and one red, on top of each other, although the weather was still hot. She sat squarely in a big armchair and looked at him. The room was crowded with furniture. At her elbow was a small round table bearing a tea-tray.

'I thought you'd be along to see me.'

'Did you?' He was surprised.

'Everyone always comes to see me. I've lost the use of my legs, you see, and can't get out. You've heard of me, I expect.'

'Well, I had,' he admitted.

'And I know who you are. And what you are. So that makes us equal. Crippled I may be, but I've got my eyes and ears.'

'And your wits,' he said admiringly. 'So why have I come? Apart from wanting to meet a neighbour, Mrs Flock.'

'You can call me Mary, most people do.'

'Mary, then.'

'So you plan to stay on, do you?' she said with interest. 'I thought you'd be moving away now.'

'I shall stay if I can. Not sure about that yet. I may not be able to stomach it.' He was surprised to hear his voice saying that, he hadn't known until that moment. 'But it's about the house I want to talk.'

'And who's to blame you.' She motioned towards the tea-table. 'Pour me out a cup of tea, please.' And as he started to do so, 'Take one yourself, will you?' There was a Hanoverian command in her voice, not particularly feminine, but full of authority.

'Not for me, thank you.'

She stirred her tea. 'You've been talking to Lily Bates.'

'She told you?'

'Not directly, but I heard. I do hear things. So who told you what a useful person that old gossip Mary Flock was? Was it Lily?'

'The man in the chemist's shop.' He had provided a short list of his oldest customers. There was another in Decimus Street and yet another in Paradise Street.

'Ah, him.' She appeared to digest this fact. 'Well, I haven't known him as long as some. So what is it you want to know?'

'For how long did Ted Mosse live in Mouncy Street?'

'All his married life.'

'So you knew him well?'

'I knew Freda Mosse better. A nice little woman.'

'And her husband was not nice?'

'I'm not saying that.' She sipped her tea with pleasure, nodding again towards the tea-tray. 'Sure you won't? No, well he was a bit of a public figure, see, and people like us don't care for that.'

Coffin pressed her. 'But then he retired. Stopped being a public face.'

'He never retired from what he was,' she said bluntly. 'Called him a proper bastard in Paradise Street.'

It was true that Ted Mosse had turned out not to be too honest, even in his best uniformed days, had run various little corruptions and been found out, but it did not seem the sort of bad behaviour that would have worried most of working-class South London. Or not much.

'He wasn't so bad,' Coffin protested. 'And then he was a brave man. I heard he saved a whole family during the Blitz.'

Her tea was getting a vigorous stirring, so that it swirled around the cup. 'I was away during the war. Evacuated. I was doing my war work making aeroplanes. Beating old Adolf.'

'What about when you came back?'

'All I know is that I left Freda a jolly-looking woman and when I came back she was altered. From then it was downhill all the way. Cancer. I blame him. I think Freda did too.'

She hadn't told him much except that she did not like her neighbour Fireman Mosse and blamed him for the death of his wife.

'So you can't tell me much?'

'I don't know what you're after,' she said. 'I don't reckon you know yourself. There's been death in that house, but old Ted Mosse is dead himself—I knew him and Freda when they was married, what he was before that I can't say. He came from Paradise Street. I was Mouncy Street. We didn't mix much. Ask his niece. Ask her.'

Doesn't like Rose Hilaire, he thought.

'Didn't have any children, did they?'

Dead silence. She put her cup down. 'See yourself out,' she said. 'You know the way.'

As he walked back into the hot street he wondered if some royal bastard did indeed lurk in her family tree. The sons of George III had been prodigal breeders, hadn't they? You had to explain that profile and that manner somehow.

Although it was so hot the sky was grey and low, not an evening to raise the spirits. As he walked on down Mouncy Street and into Decimus Street he could almost feel the curious eyes of Phil Jordan on his back.

He swung round. No one there, all his imagination. Not another appearance of his unknown sibling, it felt quite different, and in any case that creature was very, very private, only appearing when they were alone.

No. 5 DECIMUS STREET was his next address. According to the sociable chemist, here dwelt an elderly man with many ailments and a prodigious memory. Don't believe everything, he says, mind, but he claims to have lived in the same house all his life.

Arthur Ford was a tiny, wry little man who appeared silently behind his front door as Coffin banged on the knocker.

'Hello, are you the man from the Social?'

'No.'

'Then you're the man from the Sally Army about
the soup plates?'

'No.' He had thought out what to say, not everyone
was going to be as easy to approach as Mrs Flock. 'I'm
moving into Mouncy Street. I bought Ted Mosse's
house, and now I'm wondering what sort of man he
was. Worries me, I've got to live in the house.'

'Well, it would.'

'You knew him. I'm told so.'

'Oh yes, poor old fellow.'

Suddenly it was a new picture of Ted Mosse being
presented. Now he was a 'poor old fellow.'

'Come on in, I never mind a chat.' Arthur retreated
inside the house, motioning Coffin to follow. He was
a good deal younger than Mary Adelaide Flock, and
probably a lot younger still than the late Ted Mosse,
but a limp suggested rheumatism and the reason he
was known to the chemist.

He led Coffin to a bright back kitchen, furnished in
the most modern style, with new canary-yellow paint.
A bird to match sang in a cage in the window, noisily
saluting the room.

'Shut up, Daisy girl.' He banged on the cage. 'We
are both a bit deaf so you'll have to talk up.' He sat
down on a hard kitchen chair and stared hopefully up
at Coffin. 'Ted Mosse, was it now? I used to take
Meals on Wheels to him when he got past caring for
himself.'

'You didn't know him earlier?'

'No, I didn't. I was night work, till I retired. But you could ask Mother. She's only upstairs.' Picking up his stick, he banged three times on the ceiling. 'That'll fetch her.'

A bumping and creaking down the stairs announced the arrival of Mrs Ford, who was younger and taller than her husband but just as friendly. She was wearing denim overalls and carrying a bucket and brush. 'It's turned out a beautiful blue, love. Not too bright at all, I put just that bit of white in like you said and it's coming on lovely. I wonder if we could afford a blue bath?' Then she saw Coffin. 'Hello, dear. Have you come about the Darby and Joan party?' The bird answered her with a burst of violent song. 'Be quiet, Daisy. I don't think I can play for the dancing this year. But they've got a lovely lot of dance records. Victor Silvester, the lot. Use them, dear, that's what I say.'

'He wants to talk to you about Ted Mosse,' said her husband. 'Nothing to do with Darby and Joan.'

Her eyes lit up with understanding. 'Oh, don't I know you? You bought the house from Rose Hilaire. I've seen you with Gabriel. Another chap with a uniform in that house.'

True enough, although he hadn't realized it so clearly before, that house did attract uniforms one way and another. There were policemen all over it now.

But people took houses, not houses people. Surely?

'I'm plainclothes,' he said mildly.

She moved across the kitchen to the stove and put on a kettle; tea-time again. 'So it's old Ted?'

'Yes. How well did you know him? What sort was he?'

'You policemen are all the same. Do they issue you with a set of questions to ask when you train? What sort of a question is that? I'm not God. Ask one of your lot. He seemed to know enough policemen at one time. Fancied the uniform, I always thought.'

'They've got short memories.'

'Long for what suits them. Wouldn't want to remember when he was once a friend, I suppose. Not when you think of what he ended up.'

'Exactly.' And what I'm looking for, Coffin thought, is what they might not remember, the little details, the sequence of small events that might shift Ted Mosse into a different perspective. I am a fly on the face of the Almighty, crawling over the surface to see what's what. He had expressed a similar thought to a neurologist friend of his once, to receive an alarmed look in reply. It was, clearly, a sinister symptom. He scratched his nose thoughtfully.

'He was a poor old thing when he died,' said Mrs Ford. 'Couldn't do a thing. Shouldn't have been left on his own, but that's Rose Hilaire for you. He was kind to her as a kid. Kind to all kids. Had time for them. He'd take the boys to football matches. Once took all of us little 'uns in Paradise Street to the Woolwich panto.'

'He kept in with youngsters to the end, didn't he?' After all, several had been found dead in his house.

There was a second's silence.

'I suppose they knew it was a friendlier house.' Arthur spoke entirely without irony, although he was clearly aware that it was so friendly to some, so open-armed, that they never left it.

'Never had a child themselves, did they?'

Mrs Ford said primly, 'I never got to know them well in their child-bearing years.'

She picked up her paint brush. 'I'm off to work again.' She was off up the stairs without another word.

On the way out old Ford said, 'Don't take any notice of my wife. She was brought up very nicely and she doesn't like to see any bad in anyone. There's good in everyone, she always says, and so there is.' He nodded his head vigorously. 'You find what you look for.'

Coffin waited. He hoped you did. From the room behind he could hear Daisy bursting into vigorous song.

'Ted did like children and youngsters. They both did. But his wife now, she liked them in a motherly kind of way. No fuss, no display, but you could see she did. With Ted it was different.' He hesitated, seeking the right word. 'It was a sort of excitement to him.'

He looked at Coffin with large, pale, expectant eyes. He had delivered his little message well.

'I'm sweating,' said Coffin.

OUT OF Decimus Street, and round the corner into Paradise Street, and immediately he was back in his childhood, eight years old and itchy feet.

Until this moment he hadn't remembered that he had actually been here before. It was a fabled street, but for him it had been forbidden territory. But now he could smell and feel the past of that boy. He *had* been here before, and on a hot afternoon. Did he remember cricket with a bat from Woolworth's and the wicket marked in chalk on that brick wall? There had been a barrel-organ playing then, he was sure of it.

No barrel-organ now, but pop music bouncing from a transistor through an open window.

He walked slowly down the pavements. No front gardens in Paradise Street; the flat-faced little houses fronted straight on to the road. He knew well that you opened the front door to walk into the kitchen. In the old days, Grandma was usually propped up on an upright chair and sat in the open door to enjoy the street scene. All day.

A few doors were open tonight, but he couldn't see any old 'uns. He was looking for Brenda Blond.

He had heard the name Blond, Dagmar, through Gabriel and stored it in the back of his mind. Dagmar was a friend of Rose Hilaire's. Blond didn't sound like a Paradise Street name, especially with Dagmar thrown in. Surely they had all been Blackers, or Tickles or Sprotts. Or those that got to Hook Road School. Of course, there were always the others who never went to school, who never declared themselves, but lived out their lives very privately, avoiding the school officer, the rent man, the army, and sometimes even prison.

The two elements, those who more or less kept the rules and those who never tried, had always lived side by side in Paradise Street. And yet perhaps not, because the more you looked at Mosse the odder he became. What he was looking at was not a murderer, but a man at the roots of murder. A man who attracted crime. Who perhaps found it attractive.

A beautiful metallic green sports car was parked in the kerb. A rich car for Paradise Street; he looked at it curiously, noting the number automatically. There was a boy sitting in the car. A fair-haired, beautiful boy.

A yard in front of him a door opened smartly and two women emerged; both made for the car. If they saw him, he was of no significance.

'Rose, don't be too upset. You're going to end up lucky, I can feel it.'

'I'm going to kill him.'

'No, Rose, not even in joke do you say that.'

'He let me down.' She was looking directly at Coffin now, but was not seeing him.

'Men always do let you down.' The authentic voice of Paradise Street talking.

Rose Hilaire had observed Coffin properly now, and knew what she was seeing.

'I told you from the beginning that Joe Landau was no good to you. But at least he didn't get you pregnant. And it's all imagination, this—'

'Dagmar, shut up.'

The fierce note in Rose Hilaire's voice got through to Dagmar Blond, who stopped talking at once, but the last phrase on her lips came out like a ghost: 'seeing yourself kill—' The last word of all disappeared.

Rose turned to Coffin. 'What do you want? Is it about the house? You bought it, didn't you?'

They hadn't met but her intelligence service was obviously sharper than Coffin's own.

He answered the first question. 'I came looking for Brenda Blond.'

Rose looked at Dagmar. 'My mother,' said Dagmar in surprise. 'Why her? Anyway, you can't, she's ill.'

'What is it you wanted?' Rose was still aggressive, hostile; she knew Coffin had overheard their conversation. 'I've seen you with Gabriel, haven't I?'

'That little bitch,' said Dagmar. 'I told you she was trouble.'

'Gabriel is no trouble to me. I've settled with her; she knows her place,' Rose said over her shoulder, not taking her eyes off Coffin's face.

He too was staring at her. Hitherto he had only visualized her through Gabriel's eyes, and he saw now that his little friend was not an accurate describer.

Rose, vibrant with barely suppressed anger, was the most striking woman he had ever seen.

She was younger than he had believed, older than he was, but not by much. She was also pretty; Gabriel hadn't let that out, either. Gabriel had the unconventional good looks of her generation, high cheekbones with a wide mouth and slightly slanting green eyes, another period might have called her plain. But Rose's looks went back to an earlier time with big, wide eyes and strong yet delicate profile.

Perforce Coffin knew a good deal about her. He knew she was a highly successful businesswoman with, according to Gabriel, no real flair for fashion but a keen eye on the market-place. He knew she had a failed marriage with a strange son, Steve.

He knew that she had been the owner of a house in which murder had been effected; he knew that she had inherited this house from her uncle, Ted Mosse, an old man who was himself worth investigating. A man who was called an enigma in Mouncy Street, a poor old fellow in Decimus Street, and a proper bastard in Paradise Street. A man who loved children, or anyway, was interested in them, but had none himself. He knew too that she had a lover called Joe Landau by whom she was *not* pregnant. And last of all he knew she believed herself capable of murder.

What she knew of him, he could only guess at.

'I came asking about Ted Mosse,' he said diffidently.

'He was a proper bastard, and a rotten influence and I hated him.' The words exploded in the air, he could almost feel them bounce.

Before he could answer, Rose got into her car, banged the door and was away.

After a few feet, she stopped, and thrust a hand through the window at him.

'Here, here's my card. I owe you something for selling you the house. Come over and I'll tell you something.'

NINE

HE WENT to her straight away; the mood Rose was in he would get more out of her, and the mood he was in he wanted it.

But he had a problem: the card she had so rapidly thrust into his hand was her business card, not home address, just Belmodes, Mouncy Street, which he knew but where he did not want to wait to visit.

Tonight was the time.

On the corner of Mouncy Street was a telephone-box. From inside, he could keep an eye on his own house where nothing much seemed to be happening. Almost it appeared empty, deserted even by the police, but he doubted that this was so, there were probably men inside at this very minute. He wondered if he could get them to pay the mortgage.

Hopefully, he looked first for Rose Hilaire in the telephone book; no such name, so she must be ex-directory.

So he dialed Gabriel's number. 'Gaby. It's John.'

She interrupted him. 'Oh, I know who it is. I recognize your voice.' Behind her voice, he could hear music, pop of some sort, he didn't recognize the group, but he could hear the beat banging away. He thought she had someone with her. She said something he could not hear and the music ceased. She listened to what he wanted. 'Rose's address? Well, I know it, of course.' She sounded doubtful.

'Come on, then.'

'She lives in Riverwalk, Greenwich; a new block of flats looking on the river. I don't know the number.'

'I'll find it.'

'You'll probably see her car parked. She loves to leave it flashing around.' There was mild spite in Gabriel's voice.

'I'll find her.' He put the receiver down, calling a relaxed, 'Thanks,' into the air.

'OH, CHANGE the record.' Gabriel went back into the room. 'He's going after her,' she said to Charley.

'Ah.' Charley considered. 'Well, we don't mind, do we?'

'Sometimes you are very stupid, Charley. I have got to know him: he would not go round there unless she had given the all clear.'

'He's a policeman.'

'It's not his case.'

'I'm not the stupid one,' observed Charley mildly. 'You are. You think he's your property.' He spoke with the gentle cruelty he could show towards his models and which made some of them call him Charley the Knife.

But Gabriel would not be stopped.

'You know what she's going to tell him: that she has this dream, fantasy, God knows what it is, that she killed one of the kids.' Perhaps all of them, Rose had not been specific, or Gabriel had not heard the details. 'She feels her hands doing it.'

'Is that what she thinks?' Charley hadn't heard the story before. 'Poor soul. But why do you care? You want her out of the way?'

'He'll be on her side, she'll get him on her side. And I like him, Charley. I like him a lot.'

He put his arm around her and drew her towards him. 'Oh, come on, baby girl, calm down.' Gabriel occupied a very special place in his life and he wanted her to stay there. He reached out a hand to switch the music on again. 'Come on, now is this the girl that sat down next to Bertrand Russell outside the Ministry of Defence and wouldn't pay her fine, but sang a Bob Dylan at them?' A plaintive Beatles love song poured all over them proclaiming that you couldn't buy love.

'No one's as kind as you are, Charley.'

'I'm a master of disguise,' he joked.

'Oh, I know she'll eat him up.'

In a dry little voice, Charley said: 'Look on the bright side, perhaps he'll do the eating.'

He patted her head. 'This thing you heard her say— you really did hear it? Not a little fantasy of your own?'

Gabriel made an inarticulate noise and buried her head in his shoulder.

He gave her a little shake. 'Come on now, did you?' Gaby muttered something which he could not hear but whose message he got. 'All right then, you did.' The music swept all around them. 'But what does it mean? Sounds odd to me.'

He stared over Gabriel's head. What was it Rose Hilaire saw, and how was it seen? Pictures seen on a wall, shadow-play? Things in the dark, moving shapes with no faces?

He could see them himself, for that matter, but he wondered how she could.

Rose had calmed down a little, but not much.

Her flat was on the third floor with its windows looking towards the river. He walked up the stairs, feeling the heat. The treads were covered with a kind of rubber and very quiet. Behind him the heat was building up to a storm, the sky was thick with it already. A flash of lightning flicked across the window.

'If I'd known you were going to be so quick I'd have given you a lift.' She stood aside, silently offering him entrance. 'Still, it's just as well. In a minute I might have decided not to talk.'

As he knew.

'Since I know who you are and you obviously know me, there's no need for introductions. You are not my friend and I am not your friend, but I owe you something.'

'So you said.' And he'd come to collect. A debt you didn't know you had was best not argued with.

Another flash lit up the sky. A bank of windows lined one wall of the big living-room illuminating a style of house decoration that life at Mrs Lorimer's had not shown him. The floor was covered with thick creamy carpet on which stood squat, natural leather chairs. A big, unframed abstract hung on one wall, its colours echoing the cream and tan of the rest of the room. Facing the wall was a picture of a huge hand pointing a gun directly at you.

Coffin couldn't take his eyes off it. He thought she was too sophisticated not to know what she had there, but he was surprised all the same.

He dragged his gaze away from the giant phallic symbol.

'No thunder. Did you notice?' Rose went to one of the windows and threw it open.

'The storm's a long way off yet.' No sign of the boy with the lost angel face. 'But when it does come you won't want the window open.' He could see the dark bank of clouds, feel the rising wind.

'I can close it.' Rose gave a little shiver as the wind flickered at her bare arms. That summer, scoop necks and arms bare to the shoulders were what every woman wore, with hair loose, or caught in a gleaming beehive. It was the look, leggy, youthful and sexy. Rose did it well; she was just young enough to get away with it. Gabriel was really young, but Rose could pretend with the best. 'You can always dress ten years younger than your age,' she told her customers, and she believed it.

The lad Steve came into the room, silently like a little cat; he was wearing a dressing-gown and pyjamas as if he had started to go to bed, but decided against. Coffin noticed that his clothes, like his mother's, were expensive and beautiful; the boy wore them well, as if looking good was second nature to him.

He smiled at Coffin, but ignored his mother.

Protectively and fondly, she said, 'Don't worry about the storm, dear, it's a long way off.' She moved, placing herself where he had to look at her; Coffin was embarrassed for her.

'But it's coming.' He had an unexpectedly deep voice, as if maturity was not so far off. With neat skill he had managed to direct the words as much at Coffin as his mother.

Coffin did not smile back; he did not like the feeling he was being manipulated. Instead he looked towards Rose. 'Our talk?' he said. Let the boy pull his mother's strings if he liked. Then he was shocked by his own immediate antagonism to the boy. Something nasty here, he thought, and is it him or me?

'Go back to bed, Steve. Close the curtains and play some music. Then you won't hear the storm.'

'Can't I stay?'

Rose looked at Coffin. 'No.'

'So you're going to talk about me?'

'No. Go to bed.'

Coffin walked across the room, laid his arm round the boy's shoulders. He did it quietly, but with weight. The action looked gentle to Rose, but Steve felt the force. Which was how Coffin meant it to be. He was not pleased with himself for his behaviour, but it worked.

Steve left the room. Only at the door did he give Coffin a look of such sharp comprehension that any triumph he felt evaporated at once.

'Thanks. But I shouldn't have let you do that.'

'No?'

'I should have done it for myself.'

'He's at a difficult age.' He did not exactly believe this statement: to his mind Steve was not developing, he was already fully what he had it in him to be. People like Steve are the origin of the myths about changelings.

'He was hard as a baby,' said Rose, confirming this thought. She went over to a side table. 'Have a drink, will you? I'm going to. Gin, whisky? I've got vodka. I think it's the sort of evening for vodka.'

'Nothing, thank you.'

'Oh, come, you're not on duty. Anyway, you don't have to act with me—I'm Paradise Street, remember, we know all about what you police do or don't do, and most of them drink.'

'Vodka, then.'

He watched her pour it with a steady hand. In spite of her anger, still bubbling away inside her, she was keeping a kind of control.

'Of course he was quite right. Steve's nearly always right.'

They are, Coffin thought; people like Steve are nearly always right. Deep down, they *know*. It's one of the things that make them different.

'It's about the house, and Uncle Mosse, and Steve. I kept him away from Uncle Mosse, but some people seem to fly together, don't they, and you can't keep them apart.' Rose looked at him. 'I expect you thought you got a good buy in that house.'

'At the time.'

'I let it go cheap. I wanted it to go. Be rid of it. It had been empty nearly two years. Since the old man. I thought no one would buy. He'd let it run down. No one local *would* buy.'

'No?'

'Know what it was known as? The Mad House. That's it. You heard right: The Mad House.'

Coffin digested this information. It rang true, it was a mad house, he had felt it himself. No doubt everyone in Mouncy Street knew what he had bought and had been looking or waiting for him to find out. But it was one more fact to add to the picture of Ted Mosse, that ambiguous figure who was heartily disliked in one street, a doubtful 'poor old fellow' in another, and more or less mistrusted in all three. Now his old home was The Mad House.

'Why was it called that? It's not an obvious name. I know the old boy was senile. Not mad, though, more oblivious from what I'd heard.'

And yet the house had a spiritual entity that seemed to surpass its physical one.

Rose did not answer him directly. 'I heard you asking about Uncle Mosse. I don't know why you wanted to know about him but I'll tell you. He was never very nice when he was alive and he seemed to have got worse now that he's dead. A real bad influence.'

Coffin remembered a huge, red-faced man with a jolly, slightly too general smile. It wasn't specially for *you* his smile, just around you and about you.

'I can't remember much. Met him years ago.'

'Oh, you'd be out of his age group. He liked 'em young. Younger than you.'

I was young then, thought Coffin, but obviously not young enough.

'I know he liked young people. Had them around. Everyone says so. Pity he never had any of his own.'

'The reason he never had any was that his tastes precluded it,' said Rose, spitting out the words. 'Except for one or two episodes that I suppose he couldn't miss, just to try, there was never a chance. And don't say he was married.'

Coffin was silent. One or two comments made in Mouncy Street and Decimus Street now meant something.

'Opinions are changing on that line,' he said gently. 'You know there was a bill before Parliament. Only the General Election stopped it going through. It will next time.' He was trying to ease her pain. Unsuccessfully.

'You don't understand. Perhaps he was harmless enough when he was younger, although I doubt that. He had a kind of shoe fetish—always giving the kids he fancied shoes, one we all knew in Paradise Street, but no one ever said. I suppose we didn't know the word fetish.' She gave a little laugh. 'Hang around Paradise Street and you'd learn everything in the end, even if you didn't know the name.'

The vodka and her anger were combining to free her tongue. Coffin looked at her with sympathy. He liked her even more, vulnerable and dishevelled.

'So what I'm working up to telling you is that when he got silly he let anyone in that house. It was used, no other word for it. Anyone could drift in and plenty did. That's why it was called The Mad House. Mad things, bad things, anything went there. He knew. Or didn't know.'

Coffin looked at her. 'Well, thanks for telling me.'

'And it went on after he was dead. Plenty used that house. I knew that when I sold it to you.'

'I could see it was in a bad state.' It was the process of repair and re-decoration that had uncovered the bodies.

'I was going to tell you to change the locks.'

'Thanks. I'll attend to it.' He couldn't keep the dryness out of his voice.

'You're angry.'

'No.'

'Yes, you are. And because you are, and because I like you, I'm going to tell you something else: that *was* The Mad House. Now there's a new place. I don't know where but it exists. I think it must. Somewhere.'

'And your son goes there? Steve? And that's why you worry about him?'

'I don't want to talk about him any more. That's my business. But he sure as hell goes somewhere.'

He doesn't go somewhere on his own, thought Coffin. Other children, other boys? And at least one adult had to be involved.

'There has to be an adult,' he said aloud. 'I mean, doesn't there?'

'Or two.'

He studied her face. 'You know that?'

'Just got the idea.'

'From Steve?'

But she wouldn't say any more.

'And I take it you want me to pass this on to the investigating team?'

No answer, silence seemed to be built into the family genes. Now he thought about it, Ted Mosse hadn't been much of a talker.

'You *are* pointing the finger at him—them—being involved in the murders.' It was a statement not a question. Why had she done it? He didn't have the answer to that yet, but it wasn't her anger.

'I've told you something. It's up to you to do what you want.'

The storm was really on them now, crashing round the room, lighting it with a sudden savage flash.

Steve appeared silently at the door. 'I don't like the noise.'

'We all have our nightmares, son.' Rose sounded tired.

Her eyes met Coffin's. So she does believe in this picture of herself in a murder scene.

'Is that all you've got to tell me?'

'Yes. Isn't it enough?'

Where her own fantasy fitted in, he did not know. Somehow he had the picture of a private yet public killing: murder for pleasure.

It's the crime of the times, he told himself, the 'Sixties Crime', murder for pleasure. We've always had it, the Victorians must have known all about it. The Middle Ages too, what price Bluebeard? But it was hidden, secret. Now it's come outside.

De Sade take a bow, your public awaits you.

'And what about you?' He looked at Rose Hilaire, trying to keep his voice neutral, yet open, ready to hear anything. 'Is there anything more you wanted to tell me? For yourself—on your own account.'

There was a long pause broken eventually by Rose. 'Some things you keep to yourself.'

'I know. But perhaps better not.'

The silence this time was even longer.

'All right. I'll tell you. I trust you although I don't know why I should. Twice, three times now I've seen this picture of a boy lying dead. Huddled up, face turned away. Sometimes I'm asleep, sometimes I've just woken up. Sometimes I'm right outside it, looking at. Sometimes I'm inside, doing it.'

She was speaking breathily, her words jerking out in gasps.

'Always it feels real; something that I saw in life.'

She made a defiant gesture with her hands.

'There you are then: I've told you.'

So it was just as Gabriel said, thought Coffin. She really is telling this story. Wonder what it means?

Had she really killed a young boy while sleeping? He had heard it could happen. It would have to be a kind of waking sleep.

Perhaps she had seen it happen while in this automatic state.

Or possibly she had seen nothing at all, and it was pure fantasy.

She might even be lying.

He looked at her speculatively. She returned it with interest. He was beginning to realize that, a natural fighter, Rose might be down but she was never out.

'I don't see you as a murderess. But I think you could kill someone.'

And it might be him. Already ahead of him he could see that he would marry, and it might be disastrously, he had that in him, but at the moment what he had was Rose Hilaire and Gabriel and it was 1966.

He met Steve's eyes. The boy knows too much, he thought, and yet he knows nothing.

Suddenly he knew what to say to him.

'Hop it, kid. I want to talk to your mother.'

It was late before he left, a calm, quiet night now, the storm long gone.

He knew a lot more about Rose Hilaire, and a lot more about himself.

He was surprised really, but not ashamed. This was 1966, and he was going to help Rose Hilaire, wasn't he?

He had no illusions about the trouble she was in.

TEN

HE BECAME aware of the consequences to himself the next day. He got into his office early. He had plenty of work to do there. Even as he sat down, almost as if he was expected, the telephone rang.

'Hello?'

'Jordan here.'

He was already beginning to think of Jordan as a kind of spiritual weevil or mouse in his woodwork. So he waited.

'Haven't seen much of you these last few days.'

'Been busy,' he said cautiously. None of this was real conversation.

'Still looking for your lost relations?'

'A bit of that, too.' He had thought little of his lost sibling this last day or two.

'Been seeing Rose Hilaire?'

Dead silence on both sides while Coffin worked it out. 'Contact made for the first time last night. Who was watching?'

'Not watching. Sometimes observations are made, that's all.'

'Was it necessary? Who's put you up to this call? Someone's told you to talk to me.'

'I'm doing it off my own bat. John. Give Rose Hilaire a miss. Stay away from her.'

'What are you doing to me?'

'Giving good advice. Look what there is against her.' There was dead silence from Coffin's end of the line, but Jordan, a tryer if ever there was one, pressed on. 'It was her house. Originally. She had access. Probably a key.'

He had a point there, his reluctant listener admitted, Rose probably had kept a key. Any woman would.

Jordan must have felt that he had made a dent, he went on relentless. 'I happen to know that the forensic boys have found traces on Ephraim Humphreys's clothes of fabrics and materials from the Hilaire household. Wood and cotton shreds, paint flakes that match.'

Happen to know is good, thought Coffin. 'What about the other bodies, then?'

Silence for a bit, so there was nothing on them, as there would not be in the normal way of life since Ephraim Humphreys had been a friend of Steve Hilaire's and they, presumably, had not. A plus for Rose and Steve.

'You can't overlook the boots,' said Jordan. 'Rose Hilaire is trouble. And her son too, if I'm any judge of character. Leave that pair alone. I've seen a lot of good coppers ruined that way. And you are a good one, John.'

Not a mouse in the woodwork, or a spiritual weevil, Coffin decided as he put the receiver down, but the voice of conscience.

Probably Jordan hadn't really spoken at all, he was a kind of doppelgänger telling Coffin not only what he ought to do, but what he also knew. The other half of him speaking, the half that knew it ought to run.

He and Jordan had known each other for some years, and worked together side by side on a case of armed robbery, and been friends.

But friends who eyed each other all the time, not exactly with envy, but with care to see who got ahead.

The patronage of the big man Dander had edged Coffin ahead (not unnoticed by his friend), but then Jordan had made a prudent and happy marriage with the only child of a chief superintendent.

In a way each admired the other's skill at living, while enjoying the odd false step.

In the world where Rose Hilaire and Belmodes moved rumours ran around quickly. Very soon her competitors in their showrooms on the other side of Oxford Street or in the side streets off Bond Street knew that she was in trouble. Some sort of trouble, the exact nature was not precisely clear, but the word murder began to creep in.

The story about the whole bloodstained cupboard being removed from Belmodes to a police laboratory went the rounds with the speed of light, being especially well received at Teddy Touch's outfit, marketing street clothes known as Touchline.

Belmodes was not as big as most of the firms concerned, but Rose was regarded with respect as 'quality'. She had an eye for talent which they respected, she knew how to pick her designers, and could be relied on to spot a trend developing and to promote it. Never original, they knew that, they respected her position in the market-place.

But, of course, it was delightful if she took a fall. The competitors in the fashion world watched each other closely always, for any sign of faltering. They were on a roundabout, anyway, or if you preferred the image, a swing. Sometimes you were up, sometimes you were down, the thing was to keep swinging and not fall off.

As it was only too easy to do. They remembered with joy when Alberta Monterecchio went in for culotte suits in a satin, velvet and even leather, just when the mini skirt was appearing. The clothes were applauded on the cat-walk, but stayed in the racks. Ordinary women seemed to know instinctively that from the hip down (and especially from behind) culottes produced an unflattering outline, the mini won hands down. Then Alberta disappeared, to reappear some-

time later, working for a wholesaler selling through
catalogues. There had been other collapses, there were
little ones all the time, and big ones too like the 'Tim
and Teddy' shops' rapid demise (which had been simply because of their slovenly accounting), but Rose
had a special place. She was genuine, by which they
meant she paid her bills in good time, and employed
union labour. Belmodes had been around a long time.
Rose was second generation in it, and she had taken it
from a back street operation to a small, high class
chain.

But murder? The word was passed around, rapidly, almost secretly, like a small valuable coin. Cal-
culation began at once.

The first sign of this was two approaches to Gabriel for her services; one disguised as a joking phone
call, the other as a polite invitation to lunch, but both
real. She knew they were real. Gabriel understood the
ways of her world. She saw at once what was happening to her and to Rose, and where it could lead them
both. She could read the geography of a life with the
best.

She put the telephone receiver down on the invitation to lunch with a quiet face, but an excited heart.

'What was that?'

'Nothing, Rose.'

'I don't like personal calls in work hours.'

'It was about an order, Rose,' said Gabriel smoothly.

They wouldn't fight now, not those two, but the battle would be continued at a time and place of their own choosing.

Both women went back to work. Gabriel, troubled yet excited. The evening before she had talked about Rose to Charley; she couldn't believe Rose was a murderer. 'Plenty of women murderers,' he had answered, this was one of his subjects. Madeleine Smith, Mrs Merrifield, and Mrs Christofix only last year.

Rose was worried. They won't arrest me or Steve, she thought. Lack of evidence, surely. Or is there? What could they have found? She worried away at the problem. Questions biting at her like rats, ending up with the sharpest bite of all. They don't hang women for murder any more, no more Ruth Ellises. No one hangs. But life imprisonment? The thought was terrifying to one whose whole being was devoted to the outer show.

Rose moved around her factory aware all the time of the undercurrents from the women working there. A good many had worked there for years, some going back to the days of her grandfather. Army uniforms they'd made then, with a percentage of Utility clothes. But Rose knew that wily Grandpa had quietly saved enough cloth to make a few high quality, black market clothes. Not much profit came from these transactions but friends were made and contacts kept up that were to prove useful in the peace. Rose knew that she had built on the foundations well and truly laid by Grandpa. Bombed out of one small premises, Grandpa had moved from factory to factory, finally ending up in what was now Belmodes. Up all the way. There had been a brief downturn when her husband, a disaster if there ever was one, had been general manager. His ideas of management (which had involved business lunches, a Rolls with expensive chauffeur, and a succession of pretty secretaries), had nearly brought them to bankruptcy.

Nevertheless, it was during this period, just after her son was born, when Rose had opened her first shop. Out of a lot of misery, she created a beginning. That was fighting.

She was fighting now as she moved about the work floor. Belmodes was busy. In the main factory, heads were bent over the new German sewing-machines in which Rose had recently invested. Money well spent, the girls liked using them. She called them girls but many were women whose working days went back to the Utility dresses and khaki battle-dress. She had inherited a loyal staff along with the business.

But she had to keep them loyal. In these days of full employment any one of the skilled women could find a job elsewhere easily. In this area a number of small clothing-manufacturers had set themselves up since the war, migrating out from the East end of London. At the end of the war there had been a lot of money-grants for reconstruction as well as tax concessions. Grandpa had not been the only one who grabbed.

Lily Bates was back at work, Rose could see her unmistakable small figure with her shock of grey hair quickly moving a flow of green jersey through her machine. She was a good worker. One of the best.

Dagmar silently appeared at Rose's elbow.

'Bad storm last night,' said Rose absently, her gaze yet on Lily, her thoughts ever on her own trouble. 'Sorry I sounded off yesterday. I was worried about Steve.' Still was, for that matter. 'He gets under my skin sometimes.'

'You worry about him too much.'

'I don't.' That was true. Steve had earned every ounce of worry she expended on him. Probably there were depths to worry about in him she had not even plumbed. Occasionally with him she had the sense she was going down through a hole in the floor.

'How is he today?'

'He went to school. I drove him there.' And watched him walk inside, and sat in the car watching for ten minutes to see that he stayed. 'It was brave of him really.'

If it was courage, his face had expressed indifference, but his back had conveyed desperation, while he had slid through the door with his body touching the wall. If posture and where you put your body meant anything (and she had heard sociologists say it did), Steve had a strong desire not to be seen.

'I shall collect him at the end of the day. I think that's best, don't you?'

'Still taking off at intervals, is he?' With certain reservations, Dagmar was in Rose's confidence.

'Sort of.'

'Ever think of having him followed?'

'How?'

'You could get a detective. Hire one.'

Dagmar came up with some practical suggestions sometimes. It was a good idea. But she had a detective now: Coffin.

'Don't you think the police are doing that?'

'But they aren't going to tell you, are they?'

'No.' Or not yet. Perhaps never. Or possibly in a court of justice. 'I'll think about it.'

'If anyone's brave, it's you. Brave of you to come here today.'

'Thank you, Dagmar.' Dagmar was a real pain sometimes, coming out with things you'd rather not have said. 'But I had to keep an eye on things.' There were a lot of important orders on hand.

One of the things that distinguished Belmodes from its rivals was the small chain of shops Rose herself had launched. In them the racks and shelves were filled with clothes made in the factory here. Very, very rarely did she buy in, and if she did, then it was a line of expensive Italian knitwear, or silk shirts from Braganza in Spain. Something special to catch the eye, and never much of it; thus was *not* money made, and Rose knew it. Money was made by long runs of dresses successfully sold.

So her shops with their carefully designed clothes sat on top of great orders for dresses and suits that Belmodes made for a handful of big stores who marketed them under different trade names, sometimes their own, but never Belmodes. Usually those clothes were made to toiles selected by the store's own designers.

Two such big orders for winter suits were in the make now. They had been much on Rose Hilaire's mind because the buyer from one store, Morgan's of Leeds, had shown signs of wanting to move away to a manufacturer offering lower costs. Rose, whose own profits were already cut to the bone to get the order, knew that she was on trial. If Morgan's left, the others might follow. She guessed that the alternative manufacturer must be deliberately making a loss to get the contract. Belmodes must get its order out on time and impeccably finished.

She was checking the finish for herself, not a job she usually did, but today it was soothing to her nerves. Because the work was good. Very good.

'This is nice, Lily,' she said; she had arrived at Lily Bates's machine, and the words popped out before she could stop them. Niceness and Lily's cruel life at the moment hardly seemed to go. Nor with her own miseries, come to that. 'What I mean is, Lily, is I'm pleased with the work. Thank you for coming in. It's decent of you.' She had been surprised to see Lily here.

'I came because I need the money.' Lily did not raise her head from her work.

'You know you'd be paid.' Rose was hurt. She had her own ideas of social justice, and not paying a good employee like Lily because of a death in the family was not one of them.

'I should trust you, eh?'

'Yes.'

'But I don't. Not any more. Not anyone till I know who killed Ephraim.'

Rose perched on a stool so that her face was on a level with Lily and the woman had to look at her. 'I too don't trust anyone.' And then, delicately, as if it was something she hardly wanted to admit to, 'Much.'

'Do you think they will want me to identify Ephraim?'

'No, Lily.' Though someone would have to do the job. But the child had parents. It was for them.

'I'd go. It ought to be me. I'd be best. I asked to see him, but they said no.'

Rose was silent, only too aware that the whole workroom was listening to them. Lily knew, too.

'The girls are all pretty unhappy.'

'I know it, Lily.'

Lily's machine continued to whirr, her experienced hands doing their task automatically.

'They wouldn't walk out, would they?'

Lily was silent.

'I see.' Rats leaving a sinking ship; she felt sick. So they were thinking of it.

'Plenty of work around elsewhere, you see.'

'It would be bad for me.'

'They don't like the atmosphere, you see.'

Who did? thought Rose.

'They think—well, the truth is they don't know what to think. Nor do I.'

'I didn't do it, Lily.'

'But you might know who did,' said Lily in a polite voice. 'I'm not saying you do, but you might.'

'Nor does Steve,' said Rose with difficulty.

Lily was silent.

'Oh, damn it all,' said Rose. 'It's like being caught up on a bit of barbed wire.' Like on a battlefield. 'And you and I are on it together, Lily. Whether we like it or not, we are.' And I'm screaming with pain.

'If it makes things easier for you I won't come in.'

You never knew who your friends were. 'No, you keep coming in.' She gave Lily's shoulder a pat. 'But thanks.' She moved away, half comforted, half deeply concerned at Lily's information.

She felt she could not bear to continue her inspection. There seemed no point when the whole place might be on the point of closing, and she herself and Steve in prison.

Gabriel would go, all the sewing-room would go. Dagmar would stay, and probably Ted Tipper. They were the sort that hung on. From mixed motives, if she knew them.

She walked towards her office, plenty to do there which might take her mind off these worries by substituting others. There was a letter from her bank manager that had a nasty look to it. In fact, any other time it would probably have terrified her, now she rather welcomed it as a sign that life was normal after all.

The main door stood wide open making a through draught. A faint smell of Deller's factory floated in, the air nicely spiced with the usual scent of smouldering rubber that was being burnt somewhere. It was such an everyday smell that Rose hardly noticed it.

She closed her eyes and leant against the wall waiting for the wave of dizziness to subside. She knew she was not pregnant, but she was heavy with apprehension.

A car approached, stopped, a door slammed.

Rose opened her eyes. She saw a man and a woman walking towards the factory. She had no difficulty in recognizing the man as one of the policemen who had hovered around her and Steve. She had never heard his name. Without conscious volition, she backed into her office and stood behind the door.

There was a mirror above in whose reflection she saw Ted Tipper advance down the corridor and meet face to face with the police. She could see him. Didn't that mean he could see her? She shifted her position slightly.

When you are on the outside and looking in, the ways of the police can seem frightening and strange. These two seemed like an invasion force. She wished she could ring up John Coffin to ask what they wanted.

They had stayed talking very late last night, and he knew a lot more about her than she had ever expected to tell anyone, while she knew something about him. She liked him. To herself she had to admit that she would have been willing to go further than talk. Perhaps it had been the vodka working. But he had seemed to draw back. No doubt he was wise. He seemed a man who understood her.

The only way he had let her down was about her nightmare. He had listened to her telling him. In fact, she thought he had listened more than once, she had been repeating herself. The vodka again, no doubt.

But at the end he had said to her soberly that it was imagination. Funny sort of imagination, like nothing she had met with before, pulling her inside out like a pair of gloves.

Ted Tipper and the invading army had met. Ted was already in a bad mood. The removal of the cupboard and the sealing up of the women's rest-room had seriously complicated his life. He had to give up his own little hidey-hole in the stockroom to clear a space for them to hang their coats. Even his lavatory was now reserved for them.

'What do you two want? Why do you always come round in pairs? Why can't you treat us like human beings?'

'Mrs Bates here? I was told she was.'

'This worries me.'

Rose knew Ted in this mood: he remembered that he was the son of a man who had been dresser to George Robey, and grandson of a woman who had known Crippen.

She came out of her room.

'I'm Mrs Hilaire. What is it you want?'

The policeman either knew his way around or had been briefed, because he had already moved in the direction of the workrooms, followed by an angry Ted Tipper muttering about the bloody police.

The woman police officer and Rose faced each other.

'Is it to identify the boy?'

All she got in reply was a smile and a small shake of the head. 'Ask Sergeant Davis.'

Lily appeared thought the swing doors with Sergeant Davis, shrugging herself into her coat as she came.

'I'll come with you.' Rose spoke up quickly.

'You're the last person I'd want.'

'Let me go,' said Gabriel, suddenly appearing.

Sergeant Davis looked at the woman detective. 'Come on, Gillian.'

Rose intervened. 'Wait a minute. Why Lily? Why not the mother? Or if not the mother, then the stepfather?'

Sergeant Davis said, unemotionally, 'The mother says it is not Ephraim. Cannot be, because she has had a message from a clairvoyant that her son is alive and well and living in Wapping. We can't trust to that, Mrs Hilaire. His stepfather thinks it might be the boy. Might not. We believe he knows it is, but can't bring himself to admit it. That's *why*, Mrs Hilaire.' He looked at the policewoman.

Gillian put a soothing hand on Lily's arm. 'It's only a formal identification, Mrs Bates. We'll make it as easy as we can for you. Just a quick look. The clothes will do it, probably.

Lily jerked away. 'I shall know what to do. I'll pay my respects to him without you telling me to take a quick look. I've laid them out in my time. I know what death is.'

Sergeant Davis gave Gillian Murphy a quick, sharp look. 'All right, Mrs Bates,' she said. 'We'll do it your way.'

'And I don't want you,' said Lily to Gabriel.

'Sorry. Only trying to help.'

'Come on, my dear,' Gillian led her out to the waiting car.

Gabriel and Rose watched Lily's back. Unconsciously they had moved together as if for support.

'I'm glad she's gone,' said Davis. 'There's a bit more to it than an identification.'

Rose waited.

'Mrs Bates won't come back here. We shall be taking her home. Be taking a look at her house.'

'She'll need someone with her.'

'Not you, Mrs Hilaire.'

Rose looked at him, scenting a mixture of threat and impertinence.

'Because we'll need you here,' went on Davis easily. 'A forensic team need to have a look round. With your permission of course.'

Fear took a firm grip on Rose's stomach.

'Why? You've inspected the washroom, taken away a cupboard, photographed all over the place.'

'Can I just say we need to do it? We know what we are looking for.'

'I don't know, though. What is it?'

'And don't worry about Mrs Bates,' he went on, ignoring her question. 'I promise you we will look after her. We shall see she's all right.'

'When will you be here?'

'Can't say precisely, Mrs Hilaire. You understand our difficulties. But you'll get a phone call.'

'And how long will it take? I've got several orders to get out.' Rose was getting frantic.

'We'll do our best; we won't get in your way more than we can help.'

'And what does that mean?'

'It means as much as I can make it mean.'

Which means precisely nothing, Rose thought.

Sergeant Davis had managed to conduct the whole conversation nicely balanced on an edge between politeness and aggression. He frightened Rose. She wanted to hit him, and she knew he knew she wanted to. If this was the new breed of policeman, she didn't like it. His hair was on the long side too, and she was almost sure he bleached the ends.

'Oh, and Mrs Hilaire, one other thing, the message is we may need to see your own place. Where you live, I mean. Riverwalk, isn't it?'

'Yes,' said Rose uneasily. The hand was now gripping even harder at the centre she called her terror spot. She was beginning to think her heart was involved. Certainly something was banging away painfully inside her and causing her trouble in breathing.

Gabriel, silent all this time, moved to her side. 'Are you all right?'

'Mrs Hilaire?' said Davis questioningly.

'I'm upset, that's all. What is it you want from where I live? What are you looking for?'

'I can't answer that because I don't know.'

She didn't believe him.

'But once again, I promise the whole job will be done as expeditiously as possible.'

'But what's it to do with?'

'It's to do with a death, Mrs Hilaire, the death of a boy. It looks as though the body was moved before it was buried. At least once, perhaps twice.'

At last she had extracted a picture from him. A picture of a boy being strangled, then stabbed. Of that boy being moved, and hidden in the cupboard in the washroom in Belmodes, then moved again to the house in Mouncy Street. A house she had once owned. Somewhere in all the moves the body contriving to lose its boots which then turned up in Steve's bag at school.

It all chimed in horribly with that waking vision of hers.

Whichever way you looked, the Hilaires were right in it.

Now all she wanted was for him to go, so she could sit down and think it over. It might be sensible to get a solicitor. She could see she was at the point where the police might be going to do some hard questioning.

'Goodbye, Sergeant. I'll be ready.' By a miracle she kept her voice steady.

Gabriel followed her into her office.

'They must have some reason for all this,' she said uneasily. 'Something they've discovered. On the body or about the body.'

'Oh, shut up,' said Rose wearily. 'Go away and send Dagmar in.'

'Look, I won't deny we've had differences of opinion. That's style. Our styles don't match. But when it comes down to it, women protect women.'

'Oh, do you think so?' Rose laughed. 'Can't say I've met it.'

'I'm the new sort of woman. Women against men. This is the 1960s. I'm on your side.'

'Thanks. I'd still like to have Dagmar.'

'He was bloody to you, that man.'

'I'm the goat in this business, Gaby. There's always a goat; the one that's going to get its throat cut. You're from Paradise Street, you ought to know about that.'

'Come on now, Rose.'

'The goat doesn't know it at first, but learns. I'm learning.' Her voice took on energy. 'Well, this goat's not going to be an easy sacrifice.' She reached out a hand for the telephone. 'This goat's going to get help. I'm calling my solicitor.' With one hand she was searching through her address book. 'Damn. Dagmar? Are you there?' What's the telephone number of Fiddlestone's, the solicitors in New Cross Road?'

'Old Mr Fiddle has not been there for some time, Rose,' said Dagmar from the door.

'What happened to him? Did he go to prison or die? I always wondered which judgement seat would get him first.'

'He died. Heart. Just came out of the Magistrates Court and dropped down dead. He'd won his case, though. There's an Indian gentleman running things now. Greenwich 8992.'

'Well, he'll do for me,' said Rose decisively.

'What's up?'

'You tell her, Gaby, and remember to cut out the philosophy.' Rose was dialling the Greenwich number.

Gabriel outlined what they knew, and what was coming to them. She felt involved, the cloud that hung over Rose hung over her, too. As one of her companions on the last CND march had said, 'When a bomb drops you can't say: This had nothing to do with me.' After this the woman had gone on to attack her wearing feminine clothes, and somehow after that, Gabriel, although liking the woman (called Karen whom she had gone on knowing) and still believing you should Ban the Bomb, had never gone to another march.

Rose finished her conversation and put the receiver down. 'Nice voice.' She sounded reassured. 'He said nothing I can do, so to let the police in. But to say nothing, remember, that you two, and I've got an appointment to see him later today. Perhaps we should all go.'

'I don't see that,' said Gabriel: the cloud was getting too close.

'And you might tell Charley: the police will be over his place, too. Bound to be, as it's more or less part of this.'

'He won't like that.'

Rose ignored this. 'And the solicitor will find out what's going on. He says he has good relations with the police.'

'That'll appear on the bill,' said Dagmar sourly, the ever-cynical voice of Paradise Street.

'I don't suppose he'll bribe them.'

Dagmar laughed. 'There are ways. And you are Ted Mosse's niece.'

'I need to know what's going on. They've got some evidence somewhere that's worrying them. Or if not worrying them, then alerting them. They will be looking for something special. What? I'd like to know what they are looking for.'

'They won't tell,' said Dagmar.

Rose had an idea; she gave Gabriel a meaning look. 'We both know a policeman.'

'Not his case,' said Gabriel.

NOT HIS CASE, but he was in it himself, stuck like a fly.

He had taken a phone call from Gabriel, half wishing it was Rose Hilaire, but wanting to feel loyal to Gaby. What a funny, pretty voice she had on the telephone.

'How did you get through to me?' he asked curiously.

'I just kept on asking until I found you.'

'Well, you did it.' He was surprised all the same; he had been working on a case which, while not exactly undercover, was one demanding some secrecy. No one was supposed to know where he was operating from. Clearly they did.

'Where are you talking from?'

'Belmodes. Rose's office. Where are *you* talking from?' She could hear the sound of voices and laughter, even music.

'A club. A kind of club.' In fact it was a pub down in Deptford, down by the Surrey Docks, where he was a friend of the landlord, using his back room as a base. A side door led straight into a street. It was a safe house in a bad area at a bad time.

He was living on two levels at that time. One part of him, the professional Sergeant, soon to be Inspector, John Coffin engaged in a complicated, difficult, frustrating case which involved organized crime in dockland. It was an investigation which contrived to be both terrifying and boring at the same time. If crime could ever be boring. You got such insights into other people's lives. Even now he had learnt that Pete Foster, the man being investigated for murder and fraud in the Docks, a hard man, was terrified of his old mother and had kept his successful career in crime hidden from her for sixteen years. She thought he was a chimneysweep.

You learnt about yourself, too. He was always learning.

Last night he had discovered something about himself, and, as it happened, something about Rose Hilaire. He moved his shoulder experimentally; still sore. That had been part of the learning process.

After midnight, taking his careful, indirect route home from his dockside rendezvous, he had met two men. One had slipped out of an alley in front of him; he saw the glint of a knife. Then a blow hit his shoulder, felling him to the ground. Stay in character, he told himself. Stay in character. Three months had gone in establishing his pseudo-self as a friendless, cowardly drunk. He remembered giving a high scream: he was not proud of that noise, he hadn't thought he had it in him, but it had come out easily. His face had gone into something soft that his nose told him was dog dirt. A hand pushed him further into the dirt; a voice had said: 'Just listen; you don't know me, but I know you. To his surprise, it was a woman's voice. 'I know you want Pete Foster, we'll do a trade. I'll give you Foster if you get Joe Landau for me.' Coffin must have moved because the pressure on him increased. 'You'll do him for me because I ask and because he's a lousy, rotten drug-pusher. I've got family reasons for hating him. He's corrupted someone I care for.' He had sat up then, and they had negotiated. He had not seen her face, which she kept covered with a scarf, but he thought he could put a name to her. At the end of a few minutes, he had agreed to get Landau, and she had come up with the names of banks and accounts for both Foster and Landau, and the place where he could lay hands on Pete Foster. As he had finally got back to Mrs Lorimer's and was washing his face, he was wondering how much of the dirty water of the drug scene had washed over Rose and Steve. He thought it had done.

That was one John Coffin, perhaps the better man of the two.

THE OTHER COFFIN, the owner of the house in Mouncy Street, the almost-lover of two ladies, Gabriel and Rose, was living with greater intensity, even if only part-time.

This part-timer worked, as part-timers will do, with devotion. Thinking all the deeper for not being able to concentrate full time on the bodies in Mouncy Street. Three of them now, all adolescent boys.

He did not as yet know all the details of how they had died, and what had gone before, but rumour had it that no great physical strength had been involved so that you could not rule out a woman as the killer.

Or a child.

Or a puny man who would kill but did not choose to use too much force.

Rumours had it also that there had been a little bit of nasty business first. Sex-play plus torture. So you were looking for a psycho. A bit of a sadist, maybe with a touch of masochism thrown in too.

Because the other bit of rumour, and *not* passed on by his friend Jordan, none of it was, said that with one of the victims, the last, as yet not formally identified as Ephraim Humphreys, a teddy-bear had been found. This Teddy, so the tale went, had had one paw removed and a small flail with leather tails sewn on. A nasty little toy, if toy it was, and the rumour was true. You could make what you liked of it.

All this, part rumour, part no doubt fact, was at the back of his mind as he spoke to Gabriel.

'So what do you want?'

Help, she told him, and most of all they wanted, needed, to know exactly what was going on.

The *other* Coffin surfaced briefly. 'Ah,' he said. 'I don't know.' After all, it was a case and he was a policeman. 'I'm a bit short of time.'

'We need to know what they are looking for. Or even whom.' She could hear the rumble of conversation in the background. 'I'm surprised you don't want to find out for yourself.'

'All right.' He pushed a door to with his foot, the noises ceased. 'I'll see what I can do.' A man came through the door. 'I'll try to find time.'

'Sir, we've got him.' He could not keep the triumph out of his voice. He was a young man with dark hair and bright eyes. 'Parked his car round the corner and walked straight into our arms.' He was wearing jeans with a dirty sweater and thought no one would know he was a policeman. 'He knew we were watching his mother, but he did not know his wife had told us where he'd hidden her.'

'Good. Thank God for family quarrels.'

With a prayer for the child corrupted. It had to be a child, Coffin thought, and hadn't Mrs Foster been Gilly Slee when he had known her at Hook Road School?

Thus began the last chapter of a case that had started as a simple bank robbery, then extended into one of murder and fraud, and drugs.

'So he's on his way to Greenwich?'

'Yes. We packed him off straight away. Brown and Gilmour are with him.'

'Fine. You go on too. I'll follow. I've got one or two telephone calls to make. And, one other thing.' The young detective turned around, bright-eyed, expectant. 'Don't call me Sir. Anything else, even nothing, but not that.'

After a certain amount of ringing around, he got Phil Jordan. They had never been close friends but they had got on well; lately, however, a gap had opened.

He had his own share of responsibility to bear for this. Policemen are not usually intellectuals and have as a rule a distrust of them as animals of a different breed. John Coffin's historical researches into his ancestors had caught Jordan's attention. Perhaps another factor was the ever-rising star of Commander Dander, old friend and ally of Coffin and now his influential patron. Jordan had no patron, only a father-in-law.

'What's the news about Mouncy Street, Phil?' He kept his voice mildly curious.

'Oh, this and that,' said Jordan. 'Things keep turning up.'

'So I hear.'

'Oh yes. Don't believe *all* the tales.'

'Who does? What about meeting for a drink?'

This case was full of odds and ends that didn't fit together. If he could get Jordan talking, he might get something out of him.

Jordan demurred. 'Pretty busy. You know how it is.' He paused. 'Hear you've got great things going on over there.'

'All wound up. As of today. What about that drink, Phil?'

'Let me see.' Coffin could hear Jordan speak to someone else in the room. He came back. 'Yes, why not? I think I can get away.'

Permission received, thought Coffin. He's going to be allowed to talk to me.

'The Red Anchor, then? In about an hour?'

This would give him time to get back to Mrs Lorimer's, out of his jeans and grubby shirt, and into something that smelt less heavily of the smoke, sweat and beer of the Prince of Wales where he had spent most of the last few working days. Even a week of sitting there, supping at the beer by a kind of osmosis through the atmosphere, and eating solid sandwiches, seemed to have deposited a tiny roll of fat around his waist. It could not be true that nervous strain made you lose weight.

In the Red Anchor, he found a quiet seat in a corner. Phil Jordan arrived just behind him.

'Nice evening.' He was prepared to be jovial, setting the scene for their meeting. It made Coffin feel uneasy. 'You still at Ma Lorimer's? I had a room there once. Heard she'd gone a bit funny.'

'No.' Coffin wouldn't hear anything adverse about his landlady. 'Sound as a bell.'

'Not what I heard. I heard she took a chicken in the basket to the vet and put the cat in the oven.'

'Anyone might do that.' In fact the chicken had been alive but sick, and the cat had got into the oven of his own accord after a bit of baked fish. And got out again pretty smartly. 'That is, she knew what she was doing.'

'I wish I did,' said Phil Jordan, relapsing into his usual gloom.

'That's what I want to know.'

'I think we're up the creek.' He had dropped the joviality, even dropped as well the slightly secretive air of one who had been given permission to tell, but not *all*. 'We have what you might call circles of evidence. The thing is that they do not seem to touch. The first circle is the bodies. We have IDs for them all.'

Coffin nodded. 'And they are all about the same age, and they are all boys who had never been in trouble with the police, but the people who taught them and their family were not exactly surprised at what happened.'

'Yes. How did you know?'

'They had to be like that.' Anyway, he knew Steve Hilaire, and he could reach the picture through him. Not that Steve was dead.

'You got it right,' admitted Jordan ungrudgingly. 'Peter Ellis, Mark Lawrence—he was the one dressed up in Mosse's clothes—and Ephraim Humphreys. At least we know their names. What we don't know is what they had in common that made them end up where they did.'

'Except their sex and age.'

'Yes, except those two things.'

'And they were all three killed not long after they disappeared.'

'That's just a guess.'

'Of course it is. But it's what I'd expect. You can't keep a young boy hidden for long. Not alive, anyway.'

'Well, you're right. But we have not been able to discover any contact they had in common.'

'Although it must be there.'

'Unless we think of three different murderers using the same spot.'

'Like Timothy Evans and Christie?'

'Not acceptable. So we're looking for one person. And one place. One place where the boys went, then were killed.' He looked at Coffin. 'We're thinking of your house in Mouncy Street.'

'It was Ted Mosse's first.'

'And then Rose Hilaire's.'

Coffin felt an immediate need to protect Rose Hilaire. 'I've heard tales about old Mosse: how he let anyone and everyone in. How it was called The Mad House.'

'Yes. I know that; we've heard it, too. There were complaints from the neighbours to the police at that time about the goings-on. We have them on record. There was nothing we could do. After Mosse died, things seemed to have quietened down. But it looks as though the house went on being used as a rendezvous till you bought it. I think Rose Hilaire knew. We'll get it out of her.'

'Well, that's a circle and a half. What's your other one and a half?'

'We won't pursue the simile, it doesn't work.' He got up to get them some more beer. 'We're up the creek because we don't know where to go from here.'

'Is that what you've been told to tell me, or is it the truth?'

'You can check.'

'I might just do that.'

Jordan said uneasily, 'You know how it is these days, we're getting so scientific. Team-work, and all that. We use what the forensics give us. More and more.' He sighed. 'I like it. It's right, but not what I thought when I started.'

'You thought you'd be Sherlock Holmes?'

'Yes. No. Sort of.'

Coffin smiled. 'When I started out I met a kid who was going to be a detective. More Sexton Blake he had in mind, I think.'

'What happened to him?'

'Haven't seen him for years,' said Coffin regretfully. 'But I heard he was making a fortune flogging antiques in Los Angeles.' He looked at Jordan. 'So what's the problem?'

'Witnesses. We haven't managed to flush up one person who saw the boys go into the house, or even very near it. We can't place them there. We can't place anyone there.'

'No?'

'Except *you* occasionally.'

'And the people who surveyed the house for the mortgage and the workmen I engaged.' Coffin reminded him.

'Except them. And if we could get anything else on any of them we would.'

'So they're all non-people?'

'As far as we're concerned they don't exist.'

They did exist, though, they were men with bodies, energies, lusts.

'I shouldn't write them right off.'

'No. Nor the neighbours, nor the postman and the milkman, nor the shopkeepers in the run of shops round the corner. They have backs into those gardens. In theory they are there. But they are very low down in our lists. Like you.'

'Thank you.' He hoped it was so.

'Because no witnesses. No direct evidence. All we have is Charley who makes a living doing photography, and a pretty successful living it looks too, who said he's almost sure he saw *a* boy, can't say whom, standing at the gate of your house one evening about three weeks or so ago. Could have been Ephraim.'

'What was Charley doing?'

'Taking photographs.'

'Pity he didn't take that one.'

'And then we have an old lady, more or less an invalid so she never goes out, who thinks she saw someone climbing over the garden fence one night. She called her son, he's the chemist, but he couldn't see anyone.'

'Does seem a load of nothing. But it's always the way. Then something cracks open and you have a case.'

Or you didn't; he had to admit that was the way too.

'I can see why you want the forensic boys on it,' he added thoughtfully.

'Yes. And what they have told us is that the first body was too far decomposed to be very helpful. He went in about twelve months ago. But it looks as if he was strangled, might have been drugged. Some evidence of having been beaten before death and probably sexually assaulted.'

'That was the body dressed up in Mosse's clothes?'

'Yes. They were just wrapped around him. Then the second body—in time, that is; the one found first because it was on top—had also been strangled, and possibly sexually assaulted. Traces of drugs. Both of these lads had bits and pieces on their clothes and bodies that placed them as killed in the house where they were buried. Probably in the same room where they were found.'

Coffin waited.

'It's the third body, the one in your garden, that's got more to say for itself.'

'That's the boy, Ephraim?'

'He seems to have been moved around. This is what they say: they think he was stabbed in one place—tiny flecks of polished wood on the body. Then he was placed while still alive and bleeding somewhere else. They think that it was an enclosed place, a cupboard, or under floorboards. Either in the building where he was killed or elsewhere!'

The cupboard at Belmodes, thought Coffin at once. 'How do they know?'

'Mouse droppings,' said Phil Jordan succinctly. 'And that means he was in a house or somewhere of human usage. The mouse lives with us, you know.'

Belmodes was probably alive with mice.

'As well as the mouse droppings there was a dead housefly caught up in the clothing. And a slug had left a trail across one leg.'

Now he remembered that Phil Jordan had always transmitted unpleasant details in this lugubrious yet informative way. He was doing it now.

Slugs as well as mice at Belmodes, probably. No doubt an acute team of forensic scientists, skilled in the right disciplines, could distinguish between the mice and slugs of Belmodes and those of Mouncy Street and Rose Hilaire's pad. So that was what the search was all about.

'Then the body was moved again to where it was buried.'

'In the garden of my house.' He thought about it. 'Seems a lot of moving around?'

'There would be a reason for it. The place where the killing took place is being visited. Or something like that.'

'Or someone is moving in.'

'Or someone is moving in. Or there are workmen arriving.' He amplified it. 'For some reason as yet unknown, the place got dangerous and the body had to be hidden until it could be buried.'

Coffin had been thinking. 'All this activity does not have to have taken place under one roof?'

He was thinking of the places under review: Belmodes, his house in Mouncy Street, Rose Hilaire's flat. All, or a mixture of all three places, were suspect.

Jordan shrugged. 'If you put it like that, no. This is what we have to establish.'

'So that's what the search is about?' Little bits of this and scraps of that, and Ephraim's bits of wood, flakes of paint, animal excretions from the three establishments named, were going to be gathered and matched against similar scraps found on the three bodies. Then with any luck the investigating team would have some circumstantial evidence to go upon.

'Just about,' said Jordan.

'And you're concentrating on three sites: Belmodes, Rose Hilaire's flat, and my house in Mouncy Street?'

'That's about it.'

'Any others?'

'Not that I know.'

Well, he had got Phil Jordan talking, and this was what he had got.

'We shall go over the Belmodes factory from wall to wall.'

Coffin wondered if, somehow, the story of Rose Hilaire's nightmare had reached police ears. Not impossible.

There is always a point in every case where direct evidence has to give way to circumstantial evidence. What would they call this fantasy of Rose's?

He thought it was the end of the conversation, but Jordan had a surprise for him.

He offered it to Coffin, not as a prize, but more as an afterthought. He swirled the beer in the glass, staring at it as if it was tea and he was reading the leaves.

'We found out a funny thing about the kids, lads really, they weren't so young. In all cases they'd had a violent experience in earlier childhood. Seen violence.' He ticked them off like items in a catalogue. 'Body Number One, the first buried, turns out to have been in a railway accident—the one at London Bridge, when he was four. Buried under debris for hours till he was got out. Said to remember nothing about it. That's interesting, if you like.'

'He must have remembered a bit.'

'Didn't want to. Got it inside him like a stomachache. The other boy, the first one found, your body.'

'Thanks.' Even in a joke he didn't want it called his.

'Well, that boy was rescued from a burning house. One his own father set alight, I may say, by falling asleep when drinking.'

'And Ephraim Humphreys?'

'Oh yes, him.' Jordan frowned. 'He fell off a cliff as a toddler. Fell or was pushed. There was some doubt whether another child had pushed him or not. All in the way of fun, of course. That wasn't the end of it: Ephraim didn't fall far, he got caught in a bush, but he saw the man who was trying to rescue him go all the way down.'

'Nasty.'

'I wondered if it mattered? We've all been through the war. Lots of violence in everyone's past.' Jordan, although a great picker-up of interesting details, as now, had no great love for psychological probes. 'Another thing: not one of the victims has a proper father. One's dead, one's in prison, and the other is a sailor.'

'Ephraim?'

'His father is a wanderer.' Jordan ruminated. 'So each of the victims has a similar profile.'

Sometimes he said good things as if by chance. Coffin envied him this knack.

The same profile of violence, seen and endured; the same parental hole to be filled in by someone or something.

How did the victims' profiles match with that of their killers? Perhaps they fitted together with the protuberances of one party fitting into the hollows of the other to make a perfect whole.

Or, put another way, what one had to offer the other needed.

His friend had a further shock for him. 'There's one thing the scientific boys have put forward as a speculation. They're not sure, but they think it looks as if all three bodies were trussed up like parcels. When newly dead, and before rigor mortis had set in. They detect marks. Almost as if they were going to be posted. Parcel post.'

He had a rotten sense of humour. What he had to say made Coffin feel sick.

'Wonder who the postman was?'

ELEVEN

THE TALK at the Red Anchor had gone on longer than he had expected, and he still had to tell Gabriel and Rose, who must be sitting somewhere waiting anxiously.

He found them in a melancholy group, joined by Charley, in Cat's Coffee Shop.

'How did you know where to find us?'

'I used my deductive, detective powers. I rang both homes and got no answer. And then I saw Rose's car.'

'Can't miss it, can you?' Rose was half proud, half disconcerted. 'Everyone knows my car.'

He sat down beside them. Cat, unasked, produced a cheese sandwich and a cup of frothing coffee. He decided to eat the sandwich and ignore the coffee. He was old enough to remember coffee that did not have a collection of bubbles on top.

Over the sandwich, he gave them a suitably edited version of what he had learnt. He did not tell them that the bodies had been dealt with like parcels. Nor of the detritus found upon them.

'That's it, then,' said Rose. 'They have a good idea who they are after and now they are looking for evidence to back it up.' Life in Paradise Street had made her cynical about police work. 'We might as well go home and watch.'

'Will they let us?' Gabriel took over John Coffin's neglected cup and began to drink it in anxious little sips.

'They're all over my place too,' said Charley. 'The studio, all the store-rooms. The darkroom, even. I had to give them the keys. Just because I'm your tenant, Rose.'

'Sorry.'

'Oh, blame Gabriel. She got me in.' He laughed, as if the idea amused him.

'If you're worried,' Coffin reminded them, 're-member, I'm in there with you. It's my house in Mouncy Street.'

'Oh, no one suspects you. Not really.' Gabriel put down the cup, a little line of froth on her upper lip like a moustache. She looked pretty but pale, for once not concerned for her appearance but for her friends.

'Policemen have been killers before now.'

Rose said: 'Gabriel, if I'm arrested, you must take over. You will be in charge of Belmodes. Don't let Dagmar get control; I fear that above anything.'

'Yes,' said Gabriel, both excited and frightened at the prospect. 'I think I can manage Dagmar.'

'As for the shops, let Lesley Jones who runs the Beauchamp Place shop be in charge of the whole chain. She's got a head on her shoulders. But keeps her hands out of the till.'

Gabriel nodded solemnly. 'You can trust me.'

Coffin finished his sandwich. This was a side of both women he had never seen, although Charley could have enlightened him.

He felt sad. Rose's kingdom was being divided up. He wanted to say, 'Don't do it. Remember King Lear. You'll never get it back.' He chewed the dry crust without speaking. Perhaps it was not true. Perhaps Gabriel was to be trusted. But he felt instinctively that in matters of this sort, she was not. 'Can I finish my coffee, please? If there's any left. This bread is rather dry.'

Masculine intuition, he thought; these two, perhaps you shouldn't trust it, but these two between them could stitch me up.

'It's a horrible business.' Rose sounded deeply troubled. 'Those poor boys. I wonder what else they will discover.' She got up to go. 'I'll pay for everyone, Cat. My party.'

'Won't the police still be in your place?'

'Yes. I gave them the keys. But they can't keep me out of my own house, can they?' She looked at Coffin in inquiry.

'Probably not.'

'I have to collect Steve. I left instructions he was not to go home on his own. Ever. Don't want him going missing.'

'You'll find that difficult to keep up,' observed Charley. 'Where is he now, for instance?' He looked at the clock on the wall. 'Well after school hours, I'd say.'

'Tonight he goes swimming with the PT teacher in charge. I collect him from the swimming pool. Now.'

Coffin rose with her. 'Can you give me a ride back to Mrs Lorimer's?'

Rose was silent in the car, but she drove in her usual manner only rather faster. In fact, very fast.

'Worried about Steve?' Coffin hung on to the side of the car door as it swerved round a cyclist.

'A bit. But he'll wait for me.'

'So what's worrying you?'

'After all we've been talking about? Obvious, I should think.'

'I saw your face half way through all the talk. What did that expression mean?'

Rose drove silently for a few minutes. Up the hill, across the Heath to Lorimer's, newly painted battle-ship grey, Mrs Lorimer's favourite colour.

'You know my nightmare—that I am seeing a dead boy (whom I never recognize) on the ground at my feet. Sometimes I seem to be floating above it all, and sometimes I am so much inside I can smell the boy.'

Coffin kept silent.

'This time as I talked I felt the ground move. It moves, I thought. My feet feel movement.'

She turned to look at him, taking her eyes dangerously off the road. 'You believe me? Supposing I killed them? Can you do it and not know? A kind of automatic killing in sleep?'

Cautiously he said, 'In certain circumstances, yes. Not you, though.'

Rose kept her eyes on him. 'No?'

'No. I never believed you didn't know something more real in your mind. In the beginning, yes, it was a kind of dream. But little by little you've remembered. If remembered is the word.'

Her eyes dropped.

'One day you are going to tell me just a little bit more of this experience of yours.'

Through stiff lips, she said, 'Am I?'

'Yes.'

Rose leaned across to open the door on his side. 'You get out of here.'

ROSE DROVE HOME, collecting Steve, who was waiting for her, in company with Jim Gordon, the games and swimming specialist from Hook Road. Mr Gordon also taught woodwork and gardening, the educational powers-that-be liking to get value for money. Only religious instruction was denied him. He was also the driver of the school mini-bus which was Hook Road's current pride. Mr Gordon let no one else touch it.

Rose and Jim Gordon were old acquaintances and enemies. Steve had had many a brush with Gordon long before the matter of Ephraim's boots in his sports bag. Steve had always been a natural upsetter of any apple-cart his foot came near, whereas Jim Gordon was a sheriff at heart. He was a tall, burly man, in whose company, it always seemed to Rose, Steve looked like a prisoner.

They were standing side by side now, and came forward together to the car, and although Jim Gordon had not got his hand on Steve's shoulder, Rose got the distinct impression he might have had.

As they drove away, Rose said, 'Are you on bad terms with that man?'

'No.' Monosyllabic with her as ever, Steve could get feeling into one word.

'But you don't like each other?'

'He's a teacher.'

For Steve, that was communication.

Rose drove on home. She knew for certain now, in the way that mothers can, that Steve was protecting someone, probably a man, and possibly a teacher, but someone who had authority over him. Someone he both respected and feared.

As it might be you, she told herself ironically.

At the door of the flat, Rose said, 'I've made shepherd's pie for your supper, your favourite.'

'You didn't make it. Mrs Hodges made it.' Steve was talking to her that much. Mrs Hodges was Rose's daily house-cleaner and occasional cook.

'I did the essential part,' said Rose. 'I ordered it.' Laugh, damn you, she thought; I've made a joke. Not a good one, a very small one, but in the circumstances I deserve a laugh.

The savoury smell greeted them as they went through the door.

A woman detective whose face she recognized was standing waiting for her.

'Mrs Hilaire? We're just about finished. I'm Joan Gilmour.'

'Oh yes.' Rose was polite. 'We met at Hook Road School.'

'That's right. 'Evening, Steve.' She gave the boy a smile.

Steve did not smile back. 'Why are you here? Why are they here, Mum?'

For the first time he sounded a boy.

'Thanks for letting us have the keys.' Joan Gilmour ignored him. Two could play this game. 'We've had a survey. I stayed behind to say so. We may be back.'

Rose nodded. 'Very well.'

'I hope we haven't marked your lovely floor. Well, I'll be off. Your supper smells good.'

Rose closed the door behind Joan Gilmour, then followed her son into the kitchen. 'It would be nice not to have to talk about this, Steve, but we have to.' As she spoke she was laying him a place at the kitchen table, and serving him his meal. She got a salad, already prepared, out of the refrigerator and laid it on the table. Too much lettuce and not enough cucumber as usual, Mrs Hodges would never learn. Not a bit of pepper, either, unless that green thing lurking under a leaf was one. Mrs Hodges had never mastered the idea of colour in a salad, she seemed to think what you needed was a match. 'The police were searching this flat for certain sorts of evidence.' She did not go into details. 'We have to hope they did not find any.'

Steve started to eat; swimming makes you hungry, and it was his favourite supper.

An irrational anger swept over Rose, so that, although she had planned his favourite food and was anxious for him to enjoy it, she now wanted to strike the fork from his lips.

She did the next best thing. 'Steve, do you miss Ephraim?'

He paused, fork in hand.

'You *must* miss Ephraim.' She stared him out. 'Come on now. You know what I mean, you know what I'm getting at.'

He lowered his eyes. 'Yes, I miss him. We did play together, but I wasn't with him the time he disappeared. It was the day you took me to the Beatles.'

Rose nodded; so it had been.

'You went to the house in Mouncy Street together?'

'You know that. But not after it was sold.' He looked down at his plate, 'I don't know anything.'

'Who did you meet there?'

He shook his head. Did he mutter no one?

'You wouldn't lie to me? No, silence is your thing.'

So it was. Steve had developed silence creatively.

'There's a question I should have asked before this, Steve.' Only I was frightened. 'What sort of games did you and Ephraim get up to?'

No answer.

Leaving him to his meal, she went into the sitting-room.

The highly polished wooden floor was marked here and there with chalk rings, like an infection. She knelt down to look. Inside each ring was one of those pitted scratches where Steve's boots had marked the oak. Almost certainly one or two scars had had a little extra sliver of wood removed. She sat back on her heels; from the kitchen she could hear the sound of music. Steve had the TV on. Ready, Steady, Go, she thought.

She reached out for the telephone and dialled a well-remembered number. 'Joe? No, we haven't seen each other lately. I sort of noticed, Joe, how you've been absent since things started popping round here. In fact, I'd say you cleared off pretty smartly.' All the time she was keeping an ear on Steve in the kitchen. 'No, Joe, don't think that; I'm grateful. You did the right thing. Wait a minute, hang on, will you?'

For a moment, she stopped to listen, but a burst of music from the next room reassured her.

'There is a question I ought to have asked you before, Joe.' The words came handily. She should have used them before, only she didn't care to. 'What sort of games did you get up to?'

He couldn't use silence, she knew that very well, you had to be born to it, like Steve, but he had his ways, nothing nasty but cold and dry. You could kill a dream with a voice like that.

'I'm talking about the night I blacked out. The night I can't remember, the night you say I quarrelled with you and walked away.'

She listened. 'No, Joe, I was not drunk. I only had that one drink. That's what I'm worrying about. Did you put anything in that drink? I know you, Joe.'

One short sentence answered her. Not to her pleasure. 'What a pig you are, Joe. But you've answered me. Thank you. I don't know what drug you used, dear Joe, but I'm sure now you used something. And Joe, don't think I'll leave it there.'

She put the telephone down on his voice, before she heard what he said.

Still she sat there on the floor, sunk on her heels.

How rotten men could be. Some men, all men? She might consider joining Ellie Niven's women's group which met once a week to promote the interests of their sex. She would not give up her bra, however, or dress ugly. Not in her business.

Just for a moment she had a vision of a brilliant new line of clothes called Uglies. Stylish ugly, of course, beautiful ugly, and expensive ugly. If it was very, very expensive, then her clients would buy it. Her vision faded: Gabriel could create such a collection, she could not.

Suddenly she felt old and out of date. A whole exciting new scene was being born all about her and pushing her out of the way.

'I'm a hag.' She got up and went into the kitchen. 'An unfashionable old hag.' The sense of humour, of the joke being on her, that was never far from Rose's spirit, made her laugh.

Steve had finished eating and looked up. 'What's the joke?'

'I'm not sure if it is one, but if it is I don't think you'd laugh.' She sat down to study him across the table. 'Steve, one of the reasons you've been quiet with me lately—' more than quiet, she thought, stone-cold, dead to me '—one of the reasons has been Joe, hasn't it? You don't like him, and you don't like me knowing him.'

Steve looked down at the tablecloth, tracing a pattern with one finger.

'No, don't answer. A direct statement might be too much for you. It was one of the reasons.'

'Mum, I wouldn't do anything to hurt you.'

'I want to believe that. I want to believe you are wholly innocent of those boys' deaths. I want to believe you never played about with drugs or silly games.'

In short, I want to believe you are a victim.

'It was a good shepherd's pie,' said Steve.

'Thanks.' Rose smiled at him. Yes, and thank you can come in many different forms. If her son was a liar and a deceiver, then he knew how to sound a sincere one.

Besides, kids don't kill kids, do they? Not even in Paradise Street had Rose met that phenomenon.

As she cleaned away the dishes she wondered what those wooden scrapings from her floor would tell the forensic scientists. The police team had gone from her house, she had managed to avoid seeing them at work by her long session with Gabriel and John Coffin in Cat's Coffee Shop.

'You in bed, Steve? If not, take yourself off there. Bath first.'

Listening for the bath water running, she went back to the telephone. She had to find the number.

'Mrs Lorimer? May I speak to John Coffin?'

She could hear Mrs Lorimer shouting for her favourite lodger, then she heard her say in a loud voice, 'It's a woman. She didn't give her name. Sounds like Rose Hilaire.'

In the war Mrs Lorimer had been an ARP warden; in the peace she was a JP. She was well acquainted with the families of Paradise Street. They all had the same voice, she said.

She was no forensic scientist but she was a great scooper-up of information all the same.

'Rose? Is that really you?'

'Yes. Brave of me to confront your dragon.'

'No dragon,' said Coffin, casting a cautious eye towards Mrs Lorimer.

'You were quite right: I have got more to tell you. Can we talk?'

'Now? Shall I come over?'

'No, not here.' She thought of Steve. 'Let's meet on neutral territory.'

'Cat's? Or the Red Anchor?'

'The Red Anchor. I can park the car outside.'

Before she left Rose looked in at Steve. Her son was deeply asleep, one hand underneath his cheek.

HE WAS THERE before Rose with some whisky waiting for her.

She drank it without protest. 'So that's the way of it, how I think it was. I was high on LSD probably, but that's just a guess.'

'A bad trip.'

Rose gave a shudder. 'God help us all. I can't tell you the terrible sense of horror I had. It was like Doomsday. I think I must have been stumbling round. I hope on my feet. But it could have been on my knees.'

'Gabriel saw you.'

'She did? God bless Gabriel. Or do I mean that? What did she see?'

'You were in Mouncy Street,' he said gravely.

'Do you think that was where I saw the body? That I really saw it? When I woke up I was in my own bed with a terrible hangover. Threw my system for days. I thought I was pregnant.' She drank a good gulp of whisky. 'And then, although the other horrors faded, I still saw the dead body lying there. I couldn't say where, except it was like a pit, and sometimes I was floating above it and it was nothing to do with me. But sometimes, I said No. Rose. You did it. Your hands feel that body. Carry the memory on their fingers.'

She looked at him. 'I hope I didn't. If I did, can I claim it was the drug?'

'Almost certainly. Rose, I'll have to talk to Phil Jordan.' Or he might speak to Commander Dander. Rupert the Dandy, that sometimes kindly but always alarming, figure.

'I know.' She finished the whisky.

'Where will he find Joe Landau?'

Vaguely she said, 'Oh, he'll be around. In the club, for a start. Where do you think he comes in?'

'God knows.'

'I don't think Joe would kill.'

'No?' He wanted to get Joe for something.

'No. Playing games, that's one thing, the bastard, but killing I don't see.'

'Anyone *can*.'

'Yes.' She frowned. 'I just have to hope it wasn't me.'

'It wasn't you three times,' he reminded her.

'No.' She seized on that. 'So I saw something, but didn't do it. And there's one other thing: I had this sensation of movement. Like being on a boat, I think,' she added doubtfully. 'I wonder if that means anything.'

'I don't know. Drink up.'

They parted amiably, even affectionately. John Coffin saw her into the car and watched her drive away, then himself walked home across the Heath.

Several people had noticed them in the bar, but no one saw when they left.

At some time between that parting and morning Rose Hilaire disappeared. Her car was parked outside where she lived, but herself was no where to be found.

Her son, Steve, got up, gave himself breakfast, and took himself to school without reporting her absence. As he said later, she was often away from home.

TWELVE

THE ALARM came first from Belmodes. Gabriel came in early, anxious to find out what the police team had done the night before. She was relieved to find she could get in.

She could hear activity in the workrooms. Dead quiet, though. The machines were whirring away, but no voices. She peeped in. One of the women, at the machine nearest the door, looked up and smiled. Then she shrugged and went back to work.

That was the feeling of the day, then? Put your head down and pretend nothing is happening. Gabriel wished she could have done so herself.

But her breakfast had been broken into by a phone call from Charley, cancelling a work session with her later that day. The police had left a mess in his place: he'd be busy. No, he didn't know what, if anything, they had taken away, nothing, he rather thought, but they had left it untidy. He sounded sour. Or perhaps just tired.

She shrugged off the cancellation. Her heart was no longer in the campaign against Rose. They were two women together now in a hostile world.

Where was Rose? She wandered round the factory looking for her and came across Dagmar doing the same.

'Where is she? Do you know?' Dagmar had her hostility to Gabriel well buttoned up, but it was still there. Judging by her tone, she might even have transferred some of it to the absent Rose. 'I must have her, I've got that man from Milan who wants to do business with Belmodes coming in this morning. She ought to be here.' Dagmar had her finger in all Rose's pies, checking their temperature.

'I can manage him.' Gabriel had met the man, a long-faced northern Italian.

Dagmar ignored the offer. 'I've rung her home and there's no answer.'

'Then she's not there.'

'She could be asleep. No, I kept ringing. Rose doesn't sleep that heavy. You don't think the police have got her? She hasn't been arrested?'

'How would I know?'

'You know that policeman.'

'Not his case,' said Gabriel automatically, as if John Coffin was speaking through her. 'What about the boy? He must know where his mother is.'

'Might know,' corrected Dagmar. 'I never knew where my mother was all day. Did you? No, let's leave him out of it.'

By midday they were still agreed to leave Steve out of it, but Gabriel was telephoning Coffin. Once again she tried the ask, ask and ask again technique, and once again it worked.

He sounded surprised. 'How did you know I was here?'

He was standing in the bare, empty front room of his own house in Mouncy Street. There was no sign of any of his colleagues, but the door to the kitchen area was sealed and padlocked. Looking about him, he could see that tiny segments of woodwork from the floor he was waxing and polishing and from the doors he was stripping of paint, had been removed with delicate precision.

As he came through the front door he had picked up his post. He identified his electricity bill and the telephone bill (he hoped his colleagues had not been using his phone too much) and a typewritten envelope which he took to be an advertisement. He tucked them in his pocket, where he forgot them.

'I kept on asking. No good. So I thought: Let's try Mouncy Street. He could be there. It's his house.'

Not his case, but his house. It was a kind of refrain that seemed to mark his life at the moment.

'You're getting to know me too well.'

'Not nearly well enough.' Gabriel could always find time for a little flirtation. 'But that's not it, just now. We can't find Rose. She's not here at Belmodes. Not at any of the shops. Nor at home. Dagmar and I are worried.'

Now Coffin too felt alarmed. There was a feel about this moment that he did not like. A real, genuine premonition of bad news.

'No, I don't think she'll have been arrested.' Not just yet. Or not in that way. It would be no secret. This wasn't a police state and 1984 was a long way off. 'Have you asked the son?'

'No. Not yet. We don't like to worry the school.'

'What about popping round? Must be coming up for school dinner-time.' She knew he was fobbing her off, but she accepted it; she was willing to sit in the back seat and let him do the driving. She was tired and a little afraid.

'All right. I'll let you know what I find out.'

After a little consideration he decided to talk to Phil Jordan. After several attempts he got him at last on a bad telephone line. Not only the usual crackles but voices muttering away in the background. It wasn't, he thought, that he and Jordan got lines so much worse than anyone else, it was just that more people were listening to them.

Give something, get something. He would trade with Jordan.

But first he would get the information he wanted. Standing in his own house, once his pride, now an abomination. It was still hot outside, and his house had at once the smell of summer and the smell of death.

He was surprised he hadn't recognized that smell the minute he moved in.

He made a start.

'Phil? You won't know anything yet from the forensics?'

'No.' Jordan was giving no ground. Hardly could, really. Neither of them expected it, especially with everyone listening in.

'Takes time. But as the owner of one of the sites you've been turning over, could you be more specific about what they're looking for? I can see bits of my woodwork have gone.' As though the mice had been at it. 'I wish I could frame the question so you could just answer Yes or No, Phil, but I can't do that.'

'No. Yes.'

'I think you'd help me if you could, Phil.'

'Yes.'

'Thanks. So if I made some guesses you might be able to answer.'

'Yes.'

'The wood is a bit special. Something a bit different. Something they think they could match easily?'

'No.'

'No? No, then it's not the wood itself, but something on it. Paint?' He answered that one himself, looking at his own floor. 'Stain?'

'Yes.'

'But it might be No? A kind of stain?'

'Yes, that's it,' said Jordan.

'Not as good as a fingerprint,' said Coffin, 'but I can see it would help. Well, thanks. Let's meet for a drink sometime.'

'Yes,' said Jordan, sounding as if he meant No.

'Ah, I get you. Nice expressive voice you've got there Phil. Ever thought of going on the stage?'

Then Coffin stopped himself. He must not alienate Phil Jordan, who was only doing his job and trying to be a friend at the same time.

There was something about the wood fragments that Jordan knew and was not saying. Was Jordan trying to tell him something, and if so, what? Something about the nature of wood, perhaps.

'Listen, Phil. I know you can listen even if you can't talk. Do you know the whereabouts of Rose Hilaire? She hasn't been in to Belmodes, and is not answering her phone. Do you have news of her to tell me?'

He guessed the answer to that would be No, and it was. What he did not expect was the long pause, and then the urgency of Phil Jordan's voice.

'That offer of yours—I'll take it up. The Red Anchor this evening. Hang about.'

This time it was his turn to give the one word answer. 'Yes.'

As he put the receiver down he thought: Rose, I've got to find you fast. And first, before my friends and colleagues do.

Then it boiled down to one simple reaction: dear Rose, I've got to find you.

BY THE TIME Gabriel and he met in the late afternoon they knew that Rose had probably never got home the night before.

'So I was the last one to see her?' said Coffin. 'Unless Steve . . . ?' He looked at the boy.

They were standing in Rose Hilaire's own kitchen.

Gabriel had collected Steve from school and brought him home, where she had cooked him a meal.

She shook her head. 'He says not. Didn't hear her, and she wasn't there in the morning, no sign of her bed being slept in. So he went to school.'

At the moment Steve was eating baked beans on toast with easy pleasure. A cool customer.

'He says he's done it before.'

Coffin's eyes met Gabriel's, hers full of meaning so that he looked away sharply. Silly to be jealous, everyone knew Rose was no chaste angel.

'Think she's with a man?'

Gabriel reflected. 'No. I wish I did think so, but I don't.'

Charley came in, carrying a small grey cat and a carrier bag of shopping. 'I got all the stuff you wanted, Gaby. And I found this animal outside.'

Steve spoke for the first time. 'That's our cat.'

'Has he got a cat-flap?'

'No.'

'When you went to school, did you let him out?'

'No, he was asleep on Mum's bed.'

'So someone came in.'

'Rose?' asked Gabriel.

'Someone with a key. You're sure the cat was in, Steve?'

'Certain sure.'

Steve was opening a tin of food for the cat, who was meowing silently.

Coffin watched him. He did not believe that Rose, if she had come back into the flat, would have let the cat out, or left it unfed. People under pressure could act out of character, certainly, but they also acted according to habit.

'Someone's got Rose's key,' he said aloud. 'Maybe Rose herself. Maybe not. I know what I think.'

Charley put the kettle on. 'Let's have some coffee, and I brought some brandy. Hop off to your room, Steve, and don't think too much.'

Steve went, without a backward look, but carrying the cat.

'Charley, you're a wonder,' said Gabriel. 'How can you be so relaxed?'

Charley shrugged. 'Remember me? Born in a bomb-shelter. I believe they had to dig Mum and me out. Starting that way, you go on as you came.' He poured the coffee, adding a good measure of brandy to each mug. He put plenty in his own. 'What are we worrying about? A few scraps of wood, a pair of pants stained with blood that's the same group as Ephraim's. That's right?' He cocked an eyebrow at Coffin, who nodded. 'And a woman gone away who is well able to look after herself.'

An interesting man, thought Coffin, I never took him in before.

'And three dead bodies,' Gaby reminded him sharply. 'Don't be too jolly. Those boys are dead, poor little beggars.'

'I'm not likely to forget, Gaby. Drink up your coffee,' said Charley calmly. 'I know where I rate death in life's tragedies. After being crippled but below senility.'

'But dying—' began Gaby.

'For all we know dying may be a delicious experience, like dropping into a warm bath after being cold all day. Life's last treat for us.'

Yes, an interesting fellow. He could certainly manage Steve and possibly Gabriel as well. He felt relieved. Better she should be with a youngster nearer her own age than with him, who anyway fancied Rose Hilaire.

He left them cooking each other supper and drinking brandy.

A good couple. Perhaps Gaby was the man of the two. Certainly Charley's hair was as long as hers, blonder and curlier too. But Coffin no longer disliked this; he might let his own hair lengthen. His hairdresser had said tactfully that short back and sides was no longer an unquestioned good thing.

As he hung about the Red Anchor he noticed for the first time that its character was changing. The lovely smell of beer and tobacco smoke built up over almost a hundred years was being driven out by other smells: fresh paint, newly-glued-together plastic and fried food. The cigarettes people smoked smelt different as well and his policeman's nose told him they were not all honest virginia.

The furniture was on the move too, with the old, solid benches and wooden chairs being replaced with curving, light-weight new ones in bright colours. In fact, without his realizing it a rising tide of change was lapping around his ankles.

Phil Jordan was with him before he realized, breaking into his thoughts. 'Let's make this quick.

'I feel the same way.' Worry about Rose was paramount now.

'What we said on the phone was true enough; of course, the forensics don't have any news for us yet. It sometimes takes weeks, we both know that.'

Coffin nodded. He was still thinking about Rose. What state would she be in if weeks passed before she was found?

'This is a private conversation.' Jordan looked at Coffin, who nodded. 'So I can tell you that the word is that they have *not* found what they were looking for. At a first glance none of the samples match what they had from the body specimens.'

'So it's a No? You are still looking for where the boy could have been?'

'You could say so. The team's feeling is that when we find that place we will know who was the killer. It'll really pin it down.'

'Anything else?' He had felt on the telephone Jordan had a little nugget of information tucked away somewhere. 'About what they were *hoping* to find, maybe?'

'The wood scraps found on the boy's clothes suggested someone, somewhere, was doing some house decoration. Anyway, repairs. Perhaps clumsily. You know—household fragments. The wood was stained and waxed.'

There was definitely a something in Jordan's voice, but Coffin couldn't make out what it meant. Household fragments? He was thinking it out when Jordan stood up.

'Here, wait a minute,' Coffin said hastily. 'What about Rose Hilaire?'

'That lady hasn't been reported missing, and she is definitely fully adult. If you can find her, good luck to you, but there's nothing I can do.'

'Unofficially.'

'Unofficially, I'll see what I can find out. And equally unofficially, it's a pity you've got to know her.'

'Why are you in such a hurry?'

'I do have a home to go to.'

'Yes,' said Coffin sadly.

And he hadn't. Or rather the house in Mouncy Street had been taken over by a succession of dead bodies. He really minded about the house.

He had arrived by bus, now he decided to cut across the Heath, through the Greenwich Park and to Rose's flat. He could relieve Gaby and Charley of baby-watching Steve, and perhaps do some clue-hunting in the flat. Did Rose have a passport? And if so, where was it?

He minded about Rose, too. He was beginning to get the idea that he wasn't meant to have a happy future with women. If he ever married, then it would be an unhappy marriage. He could see it ahead of him, like a rock you could not miss.

Perhaps he should stay with his family history and forget anything else.

It was a longish walk on a warm evening so he took it slowly, letting his mind roam over the case as he walked. He strolled deep in thought.

On a seat beneath General Wolfe's statue, which looks down on the river and is still scarred by the bombs of a war later than the one in which he died, Coffin rested for a while. I've lost my way, he thought. Not with my feet, they know the way to go, but with my mind. There's something I ought have sorted out, I can sense it, but I need to think.

Forensic evidence was all well and good. Some cases, the easy ones, were solved by it like an intellectual puzzle.

Into other cases emotion and imagination came into play. There was the profile of the murderer and the profile of the victim and the one should tell you about the other. They had to match.

He thought about what he knew of the victims.

Boys, young lads, not happy boys or they would not have sat so loosely to life that they could come the way of their murderer. Not quite vagrants, but little lost boys. Boys away from base, curious boys willing to make strange friends in Mouncy Street. Boys willing to try drugs.

Drugs did come into this story, that had to be recognized, and no doubt the police investigating team

knew more about that than he did. But he knew
enough, because he knew about Rose and Joe Landau. Drugs were floating around this case.

It was something about the times that drugs should
be so easily come by. LSD was the new one. All you
seemed to need was the right ingredients and a com-
petent chemist. Make it in your own backyard.

So into the profile of the murderer came drugs, and
Mouncy Street and boys. Sex and death. Death and
sex. Which way round had they come, and which had
been most important to the killer?

He got up to walk down the hill in the golden light.
He could see the river Thames below with the new
high-rise housing blocks already beginning to show up
on the skyline. He wasn't sure he liked what he saw,
but they did represent homes, good little ones, he
hoped, and if you did not accept change then the human race would still be running in caves.

As he walked he reflected that he had one other item
to add to the profile of each boy. In the family background there was a death. They were boys who knew
that death could come close.

So should you look for this too in the youth of their
killer? Come to think of it, you did not have to look
far. Just over twenty years ago the war had ended.
Every adult then alive knew what violent death meant.
This was even more true of the children. A child then
might have seen or heard talk of acceptable violence

because that was what war was. Taken in with his
bottle of National Dried Milk and vitamin drops that
it was all right to kill. So you had to look for someone who had grown up with the idea that you could
kill. Someone like that might even find it a pleasure.

Absorbed in his thought, he stumbled on.

He was beginning to form a picture of the murderer and even beginning to wonder if he had a match.
No face, of course, no actual person, just a type.

A young, but possibly not a very young person,
probably male. Able to dissemble, because those lads
had not expected to be killed. Or so one had to as-
sume. A bit of an actor then, able to hide his or her
true face from friends and relations. Probably not very
close to anyone. But a householder.

He thought about that: perhaps not actually a
householder, just someone with access to the two
houses in Mouncy Street, his own and the one next
door.

And someone who had come into the district recently. This was his own view, because the time-span
of all the deaths was so close. Or, if an old inhabitant, and you had to consider this, although he hated
to think of Mouncy Street and Decimus Street and
Paradise Street in this connection, then some twist,
some accident, some encounter had set the killer off.

At the bottom of the hill there was a telephone-box.
He knew Phil Jordan's home number and dialled it,

hoping Jordan had been telling the truth about going home. The two of them had once shared a mistress in Lewisham, but only for a little while. Still, he knew that number too.

Jordan was there, and eating supper. It was still in his mouth.

'Oh, you,' he said. 'What is it?'

'When you said "household fragments", what did you mean? You meant me to guess, but I can't. Was it dust?'

'There might have been. I dare say there was. Dust is only particles of other stuff, after all. But you're reading too much into it. I don't know that I meant you to guess anything,' he said grudgingly.

Coffin waited: he knew this man.

'As it happens, there was something else. I believe there are glass fragments. Forensics can identify the refractive index of a sliver.'

It was something to think about as he walked on, hurrying now.

Glass? There was plenty of glass around in houses, and a selection of broken glass in his own house and others in Mouncy Street. Not only houses had glass, of course. So did motorcars. Briefly, he recalled Rose Hilaire's voice saying of her nightmare visions, 'But it moved.'

Rose, he thought with sudden agony, where the hell are you?

He could see the roof of Belmodes as he turned towards where Rose lived. Her car was still parked in the same place, already it looked dusty and unused. Around the corner of the building he saw a figure on a bike speeding away.

He looked up to the windows of Rose's flat. Gabriel had the window wide open and was standing there looking down at him.

He called up. 'What are you doing?'

'Waiting.'

'Where's Charley?'

'Oh, he'd some work to do.'

She let him into the flat, where the television was on.

'Where's the boy?'

'In his room still. He might be asleep.'

'Have you looked?'

'Well, no.'

He went along the hall to Steve's room and pushed open the door. The bed was empty. He went back to Gabriel.

'He's hopped it. I think I saw him on a bicycle.'

'But why? Where?'

Coffin thought. 'He's gone to the factory, I'd say. Or that way: Mouncy Street. We'd better go after him.'

'That's just guessing.'

'Got a better idea?'

Gabriel was silent. Then she said, 'Let's take Rose's car. The keys are in it. I had a look.'

He should have looked himself; he might have got some indication. 'Rose would never leave the keys in, would she?'

'You bet,' said Gabriel with conviction.

'Can you drive this thing?' He looked at the foreign controls. No broken windows or splintered windscreen?

'Drive anything,' said Gabriel, which was a complete lie, but she had always longed to get her hands on Rose's car.

'Rose ever have an accident in it?'

'Not that I know of. No, I'm sure not. Why?' The car was already on the move.

He answered with another question. 'How was Steve? Did he seem frightened?' Coffin was already beginning to wonder if he could fit a face to the type of killer he had imagined.

'Didn't say a thing after you left. He never does. He could have been scared rigid for all I know.'

'I think he was.'

'Is he running away, then?'

'I think he's looking for his mother.'

Gabriel gave him a puzzled look, then concentrated on her driving.

'I think a boy would,' he said, half to himself. 'She is his mother.'

'You would, and I would,' said Gabriel. 'But Steve?'

'She's all he's got.'

The traffic lights at the corner of King William's Walk held them up.

'How did the Cuban Missile Crisis make you feel, Gaby?' he asked suddenly.

'Awful. I wanted to run.'

'And did you feel you wanted to take what pleasure you could while you could?'

'Oh yes. I felt I had a right. I had a fantasy. I'd go into Fortnum's and try on a sable coat just so that I wouldn't die before I'd worn one. Why?'

'I think times like that affect people profoundly.'

'So what happened to you, then?' The lights changed, Gabriel pulled away.

'I found out, by chance, that the girl I was in love with and hoping to marry was having it off with a colleague. So I went to bed with her too. Insisted on it. Not nice, was it?'

Gabriel said nothing; she had not been looking for a life-story.

Right, then right again, then left onto Mouncy Street. No sign of Steve, no sign of anyone, the street was deserted in the dusk.

Gabriel drove slowly towards Belmodes. She stopped the car, preparing to park it in Rose's special slot. They both got out, looking around.

Coffin saw the boy first.

'There's Charley's van,' said Gaby in surprise.

Slowly, round the corner of the passageway that ran behind Belmodes, came a blue and white van. The van's progress was unsteady.

'What is Charley doing?'

Half way down the passageway, the van stopped moving. At the wheel was a short figure, arms at full stretch.

'It's not Charley,' said Coffin. 'Can't you see? It's the boy.' He saw Steve's small pretty-boy's face set like a hard little mask. No expression and drained of colour, the eyes stared past him.

He was no longer certain he knew what Steve was about.

The van began to move forward again.

'Stop him!' cried Gabriel. 'Watch out. He knows what he's doing.'

'How?'

'Charley, Charley!' shouted Gabriel. She began to run away from the van, round the side of the building in the direction of Charley's place.

He might hear or he might not, reflected Coffin. Gabriel had lost her head.

But he had heard. Charley came running round the corner. Gabriel threw herself towards him. 'He's in the van, he's in the van,' she screamed. 'And he knows how to drive. Stop him!'

Charley did not answer. He looked surprised at the scene that confronted him, with Gabriel screaming, Coffin silent in the road staring at the van with the small tense figure at the window.

He would have been even more surprised if he could have read Coffin's thoughts: If the lad wanted to drive away, why didn't he take Rose's car? And the answer: Because the van was what he wanted.

Gabriel grabbed his arm. 'Do something!'

'Do what I can.' He began to run towards the van. He's only a kid, he thought, remember that, he's only a kid.

Behind him Charley was in the middle of the road, also beginning to move towards the van.

Suddenly the van accelerated and shot forward at speed. It missed Coffin, who jumped back, then drove straight at Charley.

There was a thud as it hit his body, which rose in the air, fell across the bonnet of the van, then was tossed forward on to the paving stones. The van drove on, pressing the body beneath.

Gabriel was screaming. 'He'll kill us all, he'll kill us all,' she was repeating.

Coffin put his arm around the trembling girl, he felt none too steady himself. This was what it felt like to win a victory and lose the war. He knew the murderer now and he felt like hell.

'Oh no,' he said. 'He won't. He's done the job he came for.'

Marvellously, the van had stopped. Steve was sitting at the wheel. He let Coffin go up and drag him out.

His gaze met Gabriel's. The girl was kneeling by Charley's body. 'It was an accident,' he said without expression. 'I can't drive; the van got away from me. I shouldn't have been let touch it.'

'What are we going to do with you?' said Coffin. What would anyone ever do with Steve?

For answer, Steve jerked his head towards the van. 'Mum's inside. I guess she's dead.'

Gabriel looked in his pale eyes, so hard to read. What a scheming, clever, manipulative little beast. Whoever loves that one, she thought, will know what pain is.

But then, in matters of that sort it was always the same, and thinking of Charley, she began to cry.

THIRTEEN

ROSE was not dead. She was trussed up inside the van, rolled under the seat that ran along one side and covered with old newspapers, unconscious but not dead. It was this seat that was being repaired with new wood, which was then stained and waxed.

Nor was Charley dead, but with a ruptured spleen, damaged kidneys and a splintered back he was not likely to live long. There are some injuries that are mortal however hard you fight. Charley was a fighter, but this was one he would not win.

Gabriel sat by his bedside, uncertain if she wished him to live or die.

It was hard for her to believe that it had been Charley, her Charley, who had killed three boys.

'Why did you do it, Charley?'

There was a policeman at the bottom of the bed, so perhaps it was a silly question to expect Charley to answer.

'Oh, kid, there's not always a Why, just a How and a When.'

'I don't understand.'

'You wouldn't, would you?'

It was the killing of Ephraim that troubled Gabriel most because she could see the mechanics of it so clearly: the boy killed in Charley's own place, hidden in Belmodes during a public holiday. (Probably because she had been in and out of Charley's so freely at this time, working on her portfolio.) Then taken over the back way, through the back road into the garden at Mouncy Street.

'How could you do it, Charley? How *did* you do it, all on your own?'

The van, she supposed, had come in handy there, besides giving Rose Hilaire her nightmare vision. That had to be what Rose had seen.

'Did the boy help?'

'Not a lot.' Sometimes it seemed as if Charley did not distinguish between a live body and a dead one. 'I had to help him.'

'Not *him*. Steve.'

Charley did not answer.

'I blame the drugs,' said Gabriel with tears in her eyes. Joe Landau had been arrested. He had confessed to supplying Charley with hallucinatory drugs, and also to alerting Charley to the danger of Rose Hilaire talking to the police. It was this that had precipitated Charley's act of violence towards Rose, whom he had grabbed as she parked her car, forcing her to drive to the van. He then drove the car back. Charley was high himself by then. The police had rounded up a circle of drug users and suppliers. The house in Mouncy Street had been known in this casual society as a place to go.

'Or else I blame myself,' Gabriel said.

'Nothing to do with you and me, Gaby. Killing is something private between me and what I feel. We were friends, Gaby.'

She did not believe him.

'In those Go-away times that I knew you had I should have guessed you needed help.'

Between the utterly sane and the sanely mad, there is a gulf fixed. Gabriel would never understand nor Charley offer an explanation except to say, 'Better than sex. Gaby, better than anything except creation. You are a god.'

The prosaic police explanation was sex plus drugs, the one liberating the violence implicit in the other. No philosophy of death for them. There had been plenty of pornographic literature and photographs found in Charley's room to support this view. Among the photographs were some sickening photographs of the dead or dying boys. 'Would he lie to Gabriel when he thought he was dying?' Coffin asked, and got the answer that of course he would, especially to a woman. A straight sado was their judgement.

And one who did not want to be punished, either, was their other comment, as witness the way he was prepared to kill Rose Hilaire once he saw that her tie-up with Joe and John Coffin would enable her memories of what she had seen of Ephraim's body to go straight to dangerous quarters.

Rose Hilaire was in a side ward on another floor, but in the same hospital as the man who tried to kill her. She had two policewomen with her, one sitting by her side holding her hand, and the other at the foot of the bed.

'Why did Charley try to kill me?' Then she answered her own question. 'I suppose because he got to know what I had seen and how much I remembered. I wonder if he was there when I blundered in upon Ephraim's body in my wanderings? I don't remember him, I suppose he could have left the van unguarded for a moment. I've remembered why I was there. The van was in Belmodes and I'd asked Charley not to park it there, but he always did. He must have been pretty close all the time. Saw me, I suppose. Do you think?'

She was talking too much, Coffin knew that, but he also knew she needed to talk. She had a heavy burden to unload.

It was heavy on him too; he was carrying it all in his mind, the whole picture of Charley, coming into the district, moving into the disused back of Belmodes; and perhaps because Mouncy Street was what it was. But you could not blame it all on the place or on the drugs scene. Charley had to be what he was, too.

'Something I want to ask,' she whispered. 'Did Charley do all of it on his own?'

'I don't know.' But he knew what *she* meant. It was a question he had asked himself. One you couldn't help asking.

Rose said softly, 'I think he made Steve an accomplice.'

'We'll never know,' said Coffin.

Not out of Steve, anyway, who was saying nothing much, only affirming that he had bashed Charley to save his mother; he had 'guessed' where she was. But he had admitted that he had 'poked around' enough in Charley's van in the past to make his guess a possible one.

Steve, not in police custody but not free either, was in the care of an officer from the Greenwich Children's Department. He was in a small home reserved for 'difficult' juveniles, where the matron in charge reported that he wet his bed on occasion and had bad dreams but showed no other signs of disturbance. He did not steal, refuse food, or attack other inmates or himself.

Still, she was troubled. He was a bad influence without doing anything. Also, he had committed such a very savage and ruthless attack on Charley. No one asked the matron if she thought the boy might have done this to silence Charley rather than avenge his mother. If they had asked, she might have said Yes.

When Rose recovered, Steve would be returned to his mother's care, and the matron for one, would not mind. 'He frightens me, that child. I wouldn't like to be alone with him.'

In her hospital room, Rose said, 'I get out of here tomorrow. Thanks for all you've done.' She relinquished Coffin's hand. In her heart she knew that their relationship had reached its peak; they had had what was best, from now on they would come apart. She felt sad and hoped he felt the same. 'Goodbye.'

'Back to work,' said Coffin. What was work? He had plenty of routine, and a new one that looked as if it might be interesting: the murder of a whole family in a bright new Span house in Blackheath. Mother, father and two children, even the dog was dead, and they didn't know who killed them. So when he said murder, even that was not sure, but it was going to be a relief to be investigating a crime in which he had no personal connection and of which he could not be suspected. 'I'll telephone you when you get home.'

Rose was going back to her flat. She had had all the locks changed. With the old keys Charley had penetrated even to her bedroom. They had found his fingerprints everywhere. It was possible he had been hoping to frighten Steve, but his exact motives were unknown. Perhaps the cat knew.

Once the police got into the van, they found plenty of evidence to connect Charley with the murders. The forensic team crawled all over it, picking up scraps of wood fragments, traces of Ephraim's clothes on the floor, even some of his blood. So they had enough.

But there was no glass. There never was any glass.

Coffin wondered what a defence counsel would have made of that lack if the case had ever come to trial. It never came to trial, since Charley died soon after Rose went home.

JUST ABOUT this time he put his hand into his jacket pocket and found the two bills from Mouncy Street. With them was the letter he had not opened. He did so now, read it, and was so disturbed that he had to drop into Cat's Coffee Shop to sit down.

It was a brief letter from an address in Chelsea, telling him that the writer had heard he was looking for a sibling, affirming that the writer of the letter was probably that person, and suggesting a meeting.

The letter was nicely typed, on good paper, and signed L. Pendragon.

With a trembling hand he set about dialling the telephone number.

Cat looked on with sympathy, observing the tremor. 'Don't say he's on speed, too.' The murders in Mouncy Street with boys, drugs, sadism had been a thoroughly fashionable crime, really Sixties, and had interested him very much.

Two days later, Coffin kept his appointment in the restaurant in the King's Road. He would have preferred a pub, but somehow that writing-paper had intimidated him so he had agreed to the restaurant.

If the truth was to be told, he was still intimidated.

'You're not what I expected.'

He looked: a fall of shining dark hair, a pale coffee-cream skin, a delicate profile. A woman.

He had a sister. Not a brother but a sister. He was still taking it in. Letitia.

'You're very beautiful.'

Younger too. She looked so young. He was frantically doing sums in his head.

'I was born in 1944. My father was in the US army over here.' Her voice, cultivated and rich, was beautiful too. 'I'm illegit, of course, but he's a good bloke and he kept in touch. Saw me looked after; and educated over here. Then he got me to Bryn Mawr. He's a lawyer. So am I.'

'I thought you'd be older.' Different, too.

'To be honest, you're not what I expected, either.'

'I thought you'd be about thirty or more,' he said lamely.

In a kindly voice (for which, later, he felt like smacking her), she said, 'I think you are mixing me up with the child our mother had in the late 1930s.'

'Good Lord. You mean there are three of us?'

They stared at each other, amazement in one face, amusement in the other.

'I'm afraid so. I have the records. My mother left them for me, although you will realize I hardly knew her. She died.'

Coffin struggled for composure. 'How did you find out about me, and my search?'

'A friend of mine knows the tutor in your history class. Simple.'

Everything is simple when you know the answer.

'And the Pendragon bit? Is it your father's name?'

'No, I married, but alas it has been a failure. I am divorced.'

The family luck, he thought, now I know you are one of us.

HE HAD expected her to drift away, but of all the people connected with that unhappy time of his life, she was the one who stayed.

Gaby went to work in New York, Rose emigrated to Australia, taking Steve (who had a spell in a Children's Psychiatric Unit as a kind of punishment for killing Charley and who knew what else) with her. Cards at Christmas was how it went.

But Letitia stayed in touch, and together, sadly as it turned out, they had found family member Number Three. But of that, later.

He had one of her well-typed missives in his pocket
the day he went back on his nostalgia crawl to Mouncy
Street and Decimus Street and Paradise Street. She
knew he had gone to Mrs Lorimer's funeral and that
he would be unhappy; Letitia was a good sister. But
her letter had its own little shock. She was marrying
again. Was it the third time or the fourth? As soon as
he got used to a brother-in-law, he went, and another
took his place. This time she was marrying a million-
aire, and it had better last.

He was glad to see the old area before it crashed to
the ground; there was not much left as it was. He had
sold the Mouncy Street house long ago to a newly arrived West Indian family, and good luck to them.

He recognized the chemist's, that was still where it
had been. Parked in the kerb was a smart new van in
pale blue. Sadly, it already had a dented side with a
broken window. It brought back so much of the past;
Gabriel, Rose and Steve, Charley, the whole 1960s
scene.

He needed some toothpaste so he went into the
chemist's.

Inside it looked a bit old-fashioned, as if the style
had been set by the Festival of Britain and never
changed.

A tall man stood behind the counter; he was wearing a neat white coat.

He seemed buttoned into everything a shade too tightly. The old-fashioned word natty came into Coffin's mind. Neat, self-contained and a bit too pleased with himself.

'Toothpaste, please.' He named the brand.

'Here you are, sir.' He had a deep, sweet voice.

Memories began to roll, like a film you'd forgotten but remembered better with every frame.

'Weren't you a friend of Charley's?'

'Charley? Charley who?'

Something in the way he said it made Coffin sure he was right.

'He had a place at the back of Belmodes.'

The man licked his lips as if they were dry. 'I remember Belmodes, of course. That's been gone a long time now. But not your friend. Charley, did you say?'

Liar, thought Coffin.

From above an old woman's voice called. 'Son, son, I want my tea.'

Coffin said. 'Your mother? If she's the lady I remember, she must be about a hundred now.' The old lady who had seen *something* from her window, all those years ago.

'So she is, isn't she, Mr Harry, sir?'

A young lad had come into the shop. He looked clean, childish and very taking. Vulnerable. Coffin wanted to say, Run away, laddie, this is dangerous territory.

'Anything you want me to do, Mr Harry? For your mother or anything? I'm ready. Otherwise I'll go straight out with the deliveries.'

'Thank you, Ron. Nothing special just now.'

'See you knocked the van. You are hopeless, Mr Harry. No car's safe with you.'

The voice from upstairs came again. 'Son, son, I want you.'

'Coming, Mother.' Harry Lindsay pushed some coins across the counter. 'Your change, sir. Sorry I could not help about your friend.' He turned and walked upstairs.

Coffin took his toothpaste and walked out of the shop.

Drugs, glass, a chemist, and, whatever he said, a friend of Charley's. Didn't it all make you think?

'I always knew there were two of them in it,' he said aloud.

BARBARA PAUL

IN-Laws and Outlaws

Gillian Clifford, once a Decker in-law, returns to the family fold to comfort Raymond's widow, Connie. Clearly, the family is worried. Who hates the Deckers enough to kill them?

And as the truth behind the murder becomes shockingly clear, Gillian realizes that once a Decker, always a Decker—a position she's discovering can be most precarious indeed.

A Sheila Travis Mystery

MURDER

at Markham

First Time in Paperback

PATRICIA HOUCK SPRINKLE

The body of beautiful bad girl Melanie Forbes is found wrapped in an Oriental rug in an unused basement storeroom of Chicago's elite school of diplomacy, the Markham Institute.

Sheila Travis, new administrative assistant to the president, has years of diplomatic experience behind her. Though unfamiliar with the protocol for dealing with a murder in one's new workplace, her nose for crime pulls Sheila—and her eccentric Aunt Mary—into the investigation.

"A delightful new sleuth makes her debut here."

—*Publishers Weekly*

First Time in Paperback

MIRIAM BORGENICHT

*A tragedy turns into a living nightmare when health
counselor Linda Stewart's adopted infant daughter is
legally reclaimed by the baby's natural teenage mother—
and both are found dead two days later.*

*Linda's agonizing grief is channeled into a burning
determination to solve these senseless murders. While
suspicions of drug involvement might explain the sudden
fortune the young mother had acquired, Linda's subtle
probing takes a seedy turn into black-market adoptions.*

*"Borgenicht's perceptive comments on troubling social
issues generate plenty of tension."* —Publishers Weekly

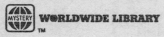